"When's the last t[ime] somebody who ca[res about you?"]

She asked gently, even as she was painfully afraid she knew the answer.

"It doesn't matter. I don't need anybody."

"I don't believe you. And it's too bad, because you have me."

His eyes tracked over her face, lingering at her mouth, his own working slightly. She knew what was about to happen. And this time she didn't step away.

KERRY CONNOR

STRANGER IN A SMALL TOWN

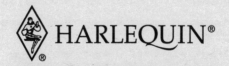

HARLEQUIN®

TORONTO • NEW YORK • LONDON
AMSTERDAM • PARIS • SYDNEY • HAMBURG
STOCKHOLM • ATHENS • TOKYO • MILAN • MADRID
PRAGUE • WARSAW • BUDAPEST • AUCKLAND

For my grandfather

Recycling programs for this product may not exist in your area.

ISBN-13: 978-0-373-74528-9

STRANGER IN A SMALL TOWN

ABOUT THE AUTHOR

A lifelong mystery reader, Kerry Connor first discovered romantic suspense by reading Harlequin Intrigue books and is thrilled to be writing for the line. Kerry lives and writes in New York.

Books by Kerry Connor

Don't miss any of our special offers. Write to us at the following address for information on our newest releases.

Harlequin Reader Service
U.S.: 3010 Walden Ave., P.O. Box 1325, Buffalo, NY 14269
Canadian: P.O. Box 609, Fort Erie, Ont. L2A 5X3

CAST OF CHARACTERS

Maggie Harper—Her determination to restore an infamous old house puts her at odds with an entire town—and a killer who would do anything to stop her.

John Samuels—The stranger in town offers Maggie his help—but not the truth about his identity or his motives.

Greg and Emily Ross—Their murders continue to cast a long shadow over the town where they lived—and died.

Annie Madsen—Maggie's closest friend in town. Even she disapproves of Maggie's plans for the house.

Irene Graham—Annie's mother is full of answers. Are they the ones Maggie is looking for?

Dalton Sterling—The builder wants Maggie's house. How far will he go to get it?

Clay Howell—He doesn't like people who ask questions about the Rosses.

Janet Howell—A woman who seems to be keeping secrets. Her own or someone else's?

Paul Winslow—A man whose temper hasn't calmed in thirty years.

Teri Winslow—The babysitter was close to the Rosses. Does she possess information that could lead Maggie to the truth?

Prologue

In the dark of night, the house appeared no different from the others on the street. The lack of lights masked its details, making it nothing more than another shapeless silhouette on the block. The trees bracketing the property provided concealing shadows that hid the rest of the lot from view.

It was only when the clouds briefly parted, allowing the pale moonlight to shine down upon it, that it became clear just how different this house was. Several of its windows had cardboard covering jagged, gaping holes in the glass. The roof sagged in more than one place, as did the railing on the wide front porch. Its front lawn was patchy and choked with weeds. Without the sheltering darkness, it was obvious that unlike every other house on this quiet residential street, this one hadn't been occupied for some time.

Nearly thirty years now. Ever since the murders.

No one wanted to live in a place where two people had been brutally killed. Few even wanted to look at it, preferring to ignore its existence entirely, as though it would be so easy to forget what had happened within its walls.

For others, such blissful ignorance wasn't possible.

Standing in the shadows on the other side of the street, a lone figure stared at the structure and imagined what it would be like to watch the house burn to the ground.

It wouldn't take much. Perhaps only a single match. A flick of the wrist to create the flame and another to toss it into the building. Then it would be done. A house that old, that decaying, would likely go up in an instant and burn just as quickly. It would happen so fast no one would be able to stop it. Not the neighbors who did their best to ignore the house's existence and had no interest in seeing it remain standing. Not the volunteer firefighters who would take their time coming to a vacant house no one cared about. Not even the woman currently sleeping inside, the woman whose stubborn, ridiculous insistence on trying to restore the house had brought back so many painful memories.

It should have been done years ago. Only the fear of being caught, of returning to the scene of the crime, had prevented it.

But now, no matter how fierce the need to avoid it, it was impossible not to return. Night after night. A compulsion that would remain as long as the house stood, as long as there was somewhere to return to.

No. Determination surged, hard and desperate and unrelenting. It had to end.

The woman had proven difficult to scare off so far. That would change. No matter what it took.

The woman had to be stopped. The house had to be destroyed.

Only then would it be possible to forget exactly what had happened here.

And why.

Chapter One

2:00 a.m.

Maggie didn't have to check her watch to know what time it was. She'd felt every minute ticking away from the moment she'd crawled into the sleeping bag and settled in for the night.

Staring into the darkness, she waited. Not for sleep.

For trouble.

She didn't know what form it would arrive in. The shattering of glass. A beam of light piercing the dark. A floorboard creaking from the weight of a foot that shouldn't be there.

So she waited. For one of them. For all of them. For the trouble she knew deep in her bones would be coming eventually. It was the entire reason she was here, on the living-room floor of this decrepit old house, when she could be in an actual bed in more comfortable surroundings. To catch the vandal responsible for the damage the house had suffered the past two weeks.

The silence echoed around her. The wind knocked at the windows, rattling the glass or whistling through holes in the tape holding the cardboard in place over the broken ones.

Another minute ticked by. Then another.

The moments that passed without incident provided no relief. Her tension grew the longer she waited, her certainty rising.

It was possible that her presence had scared off whoever was responsible for the damage. The broken windows. The cut electrical line. Anyone who saw her truck parked out front would know she was here right now, waiting for them, ready to catch them. Could driving them away really be that simple?

She'd like to think so. But she didn't. The town's obsession with the house and what had happened here was even creepier than the event itself. She'd endured too many comments, too many pointed glances, over the past few weeks to think they'd be so easily dissuaded. They wanted her to give up, they wanted her out of the house. If anything, they might like the idea of acting when she was here, causing havoc under her very nose.

Not tonight. Not on my watch.

Maggie clenched her fists tightly and listened even closer, determined not to miss the telltale noise when it came.

She heard nothing. Only the whistle of the wind and the empty, endless silence echoing around her.

That didn't mean there wasn't someone out there. But if there was, the person was managing to move with the utmost stealth, not making a single revealing sound.

Like a killer had once done, stalking the halls in the middle of the night to claim two victims.

And like them, she wouldn't even know anybody was here until it was too late.

A burst of emotion made her lurch upright, her heart suddenly pounding in her chest. She threw the top of the sleeping bag aside and climbed to her feet, eyes scanning every inch of the darkness, unable to sit still any longer as the feeling hammered through her veins.

She wanted to believe it was annoyance. It felt too much like fear.

"Damn it," she muttered, quickly sucking in a breath. She was letting the townspeople's comments get to her, and that was the last thing she could do. Someone had to be sane in this town.

The Murder House. Nobody wants it to stay standing. Ought to just tear it down.

"The hell I will," Maggie grumbled.

Her breathing continued to come in rapid, shallow gasps. Trying to calm her racing heart, she moved to the front window and peered out.

Not that she could see much. It was a cloudy September night, with the moon barely making an appearance. There was no house directly opposite, though there was a streetlamp, one which should be illuminating both this stretch of road and the house. When she first arrived in town, she'd discovered the bulb had been broken, the only one on the street that was. Despite her best efforts to have the town replace it, nothing had been done. As much as it irritated her, she suspected they were right not to waste their time. She would bet anything the light had been broken deliberately, much like the front porch light she'd replaced herself last week had been busted. Twice.

Nobody in Fremont, Pennsylvania, wanted to look at the Murder House, any more than they wanted to see it restored.

Well, that's just too bad, she thought.

She was about to move away from the window when something grabbed her attention out of the corner of her vision. Something barely visible. Something that most definitely should not be there.

Or someone.

She froze, her gaze pinned in the darkness across the street. Her tension returned in a burst as she tried to absorb the sudden certainty of what she'd seen.

Her breath caught in her throat.

Someone was out there.

As soon as she thought it, she felt a flicker of doubt, as the figure she thought she'd seen disappeared from view. It may have been the shifting light, the clouds moving to cover the moon and blocking its glow. She narrowed her gaze and peered closer into the darkness on the other side of the street, trying to convince herself it hadn't simply been a trick of the light.

Gradually, she thought she spotted the faint silhouette. The figure was so hazy and indistinct it barely seemed to be there. Almost like a—

A chill rolled slowly down her spine, like a cold finger being dragged along her bare skin.

Almost like a ghost.

She immediately shook off the idea, annoyed by the thought. She was letting the townspeople's ghoulish obsession with the house get to her.

The house might have many problems. No one ever claimed being haunted was one of them.

No, the person out there was real. Which raised the question of why someone would be standing outside in the middle of the night, staring at the house.

Several explanations came to mind, none of them good. Was he planning something, the trouble she'd been expecting all night? Or did he know she was watching, and this was some new intimidation tactic to drive her out of here and convince her to sell so they could tear down the house, the way they wanted to?

Her annoyance exploded into full-blown anger, shock waves of fury surging from the pit of her belly to every inch of her body. She'd had enough. Whatever they were planning, she wasn't going to wait for them to start to put an end to it.

Before she could even think about it, she grabbed the wooden baseball bat she'd found abandoned in one of the upstairs rooms and threw the door open.

She'd barely set one foot outside when she yelled out. "Hey!"

She almost expected her sudden appearance to be enough to scare him off, sending him running off into the night. Instead, the person didn't move at all as she pounded down the steps and stalked across the lawn toward the street. As she came closer, she spotted the outline of a vehicle behind him. A pickup truck. The figure was standing in front of the driver's side door.

She was halfway to him before it hit her just how foolish she was being. She might have a baseball bat, but he could have a gun for all she knew. He might not even be alone. It could be an ambush.

She felt a flicker of relief when he didn't reach for a weapon. He didn't react at all, simply watching her approach, as if she wasn't waving a bat and yelling at him.

And then they were mere feet apart. She had to force herself to slow to avoid slamming right into him, skidding to a halt far less gracefully than she would have liked. He was at least a half foot taller than she was, and she had to crane her head to look into his face. Or at least where she assumed his face must be. It was so dark she couldn't make out his features. She only knew he was big, his silhouette that of a large, muscular man.

She wasn't exactly tiny, but she also knew enough to be wary of a man—a stranger—his size. She braced her hands on the bat, ready to swing at the slightest indication of an attack.

"What do you think you're doing?" she demanded.

He took his time answering. From the tilt of his head, he was staring down at her in the dark. She wondered if he could make out her features any more clearly than she could his. In case he could, she hardened her expression, not about to let him think she was the least bit scared or intimidated. She tried to ignore the way her heart was jackhammering in her chest.

"Nothing," he said, his voice low and deep and annoyingly unconcerned. "Is that a crime?"

"It is if that nothing turns into something. Like breaking a few windows?"

Again he said nothing for a long moment. "I'm guessing you've had some trouble around here."

"And I bet you don't know anything about that."

"Only what you just told me."

"Then what are you doing here?"

After a beat, this time he did reach into his jacket. She automatically tightened her grip on the bat, ready to strike if she saw even a hint of a weapon. Would she even be able to in the dark? Or would she only see when it was too late?

It was the sound—paper crinkling—that told her what he was pulling out rather than the sight of it in his hand. "I came about this ad."

She didn't have to ask what ad he meant. There was only one he could mean, especially given the size of the paper she could barely make out. It was the flyer she'd placed around town, advertising for someone to help her work on the house. When she hadn't received any responses, she'd gone farther out, posting it at the gas stations on the roads into town and the truck stop even farther. It hadn't helped.

Despite the lack of jobs in the area that should have left her with plenty of takers, she'd had none. The house's reputation was too well-known. As she'd learned from her first day in town, no one wanted this house restored but her.

She gaped at him in disbelief. "You came here in the middle of the night to apply for a job?"

"I came here in the middle of the night because that's when I got into town," he said as though it were the most logical thing in the world. "It didn't seem worth trying to get a motel room for what's left of the night, so I figured I'd camp out in the truck until morning. It's not the first time."

It was the kind of thing some people might have judged him for, the idea that he'd slept in his truck in the past. Some might wonder if he were homeless. Maggie had worked in the restoration business too long, worked with too many guys who were just passing through, to find it unusual.

"Where'd you get the flyer?"

"The truck stop," he said. "I wasn't planning on stopping, but I could use the work and it seemed like as good an opportunity as any. Thought I might as well check it out."

On the surface, his words made sense. Given the circumstances, not to mention everything she'd put up with the past several weeks, she couldn't entirely brush away her wariness. "What exactly is your background? Have you worked construction before?"

"Yep. Done a little bit of everything. Whatever paid the bills."

The words were plain-spoken, his tone even. If he was a liar, he was a good one. She just couldn't figure out why he would be lying, why he would be there with that flyer at this time of night for any reason but the one he'd stated.

She wished again that she could see his face. Just a glimpse. The moon offered no help, remaining stubbornly hidden behind the clouds. He was little more than a dark shadow looming over her.

"What's your name?" she asked.

"John," he said. "John…Samuels."

He'd answered slowly again, taking his time before providing his first name. If she hadn't been listening closely, she might have missed the slight beat before he offered his last, as well.

That slight hesitation, so brief she might have imagined it, made her hold on to the last bit of wariness she'd been about to relinquish. Why the pause? Because that wasn't really his name? Or was she simply imagining what she thought she'd heard, her instincts so on edge because of everything that had happened lately she was reading things that weren't there?

Whatever the case, she wasn't exactly in the right frame of mind to be interviewing a job applicant. It was two in the morning and she was standing in the dark in nothing but a T-shirt and sweatpants, talking to a complete stranger whose face she couldn't even see.

The man might be trouble, but not the immediate kind. She could wait to deal with him in the morning.

"Well, John Samuels," she said. "As you can imagine I wasn't expecting any job applicants right now. We can talk about it in the morning. That is, if I haven't scared you off the idea of working for me."

"I don't scare that easily."

That was reassuring. Given the number of people who'd probably try to warn him off if he took the job, it was a good quality to have.

"Okay, then," she said. "I guess I'll see you in the morning."

There was a flash of motion that might have been him nodding. "Sounds good."

Maggie slowly backed away, not quite ready to let down her guard. Only when she was on the other side of the street did she finally turn. She marched back to the house, glancing over her shoulder at him every few steps. He never moved her entire way there. She could feel his eyes on her, hot and unrelenting.

Finally reaching the house, she hurried up the steps and rushed inside. She closed the door behind herself and locked it, then sagged against it. She drew in a breath, once again trying to slow her suddenly racing heart.

That had certainly been odd.

Considering the circumstances, she wouldn't blame the man if he was nowhere to be found when morning came. Despite his words, she had to believe anyone would have second thoughts about working for someone who introduced herself by coming at him with a baseball bat. A reluctant chuckle worked its way from her lungs. And after all the trouble he'd gone to to find the place at this time of night—

The laugh died in her throat. Only then did it occur to her that the address hadn't been listed on the flyer. At this time of night, nothing would have been open in town, so no one would have been around to give him directions.

So how had he known how to find the house?

The thought drove her back to the window.

He was nowhere in sight. There was nothing there.

It was like he'd never been there at all.

She scanned the darkness frantically, her heart in her throat, the notion that she'd somehow imagined the encounter leaping to mind.

Then she spotted it. The silhouette of his truck, barely visible but unmistakably there.

She slowly relaxed, her shoulders slumping, even if the emotion coursing through her couldn't quite be described as relief. Instead, her wariness was back, tugging insistently deep within her.

She stared at the truck's faint outline, almost tempted to go out there and confront him. Embarrassment held her in place. She'd already made a fool of herself once tonight by asking a question he'd had a reasonable enough answer for. She didn't really feel like risking having the same thing happen again.

Whatever the answer was, it could wait until morning. She could find out then.

And she would, she thought resolutely, turning

away from the window to scan the darkness of the house. She'd dealt with enough nonsense when it came to this house.

Whether it came from the man outside or any number of vandals, she wasn't going to put up with any more.

SAM watched the woman make her way back to the house. Every few steps she'd stop and he sensed her glancing back at him, but he couldn't see her face any more than he suspected she could see his. A minute later, she finally reached the house and slipped inside.

For what seemed like the first time since she'd come tearing out of the building, yelling and brandishing a bat, he took a breath.

It hadn't exactly been how he'd wanted his first meeting with his intended boss to go. He'd have to work hard to make a better impression in the morning. He needed this job. It was too perfect for his purposes. In a town this small, there was little reason for a stranger to show up for no reason and stick around.

And he wasn't going anywhere.

Pulling open the door of the truck, he climbed back into the driver's seat. He probably should have stayed there in the first place rather than getting out and standing in the open. No wonder he'd caught her attention. Naturally, she'd be suspicious of a stranger standing in the dark in the middle of the night staring at her house.

But after the long drive, he'd needed to stretch his legs. Not to mention, he'd wanted to try to get a better look at the house. It was so dark he hadn't been able to see much from the truck. He'd thought he might have a better chance of seeing the house from outside.

To see if it matched what he saw in his nightmares.

Even as he thought it, the image rose in his mind, not the building shadowed in darkness, but the one he remembered. A shudder rolled through him, causing his limbs to jerk, the motion completely involuntary.

A ragged breath worked its way from his lungs. He'd never thought he'd be here again, never wanted to return to this town, let alone this house. But here he was.

And this was only the beginning.

Tomorrow he'd have to gain the woman's trust, get her to hire him. Then he'd have to walk into that house.

The thought of it damn near sent another jolt through him. He somehow managed to keep his reaction in check.

In the next few days he was going to have to do more than walk into that house. He was going to have to face every aspect of the past head-on. No matter how much the idea terrified him. No matter how much pain it threatened to cause. No matter how many people in this little town wanted to forget the past, just as much as he did.

Until he finally had the truth.

No matter what it cost him.

Chapter Two

After a nearly sleepless night spent waiting for trouble that never arrived, Maggie really would have liked to see a friendly face first thing in the morning.

The man climbing out of the car he'd parked behind her truck most certainly did not qualify.

Gritting her teeth, Maggie fought the urge to turn around, walk back up the steps she'd just come down and go back inside. She knew better than to think Dalton Sterling would be so easily put off. In his early seventies, the builder had the demeanor of someone who'd spent his life getting his own way, and he'd been a pain from virtually the first moment she arrived in town. Even if she were the kind of woman to run and hide, she figured he'd just follow. He wasn't going to give up until he got what he wanted.

Too bad there wasn't a chance in hell she was going to give it to him.

Spotting her, he raised a hand, a phony smile stretching across his face. "Morning, Maggie. I was surprised to hear you'd checked out of the motel."

Folding her arms over her chest, she raised a brow. "Checking up on me, Dalton?"

He walked up to her. "It's a small town. People look out for each other around here."

"Are you really looking out for me, or for your own interests?"

"As far as I'm concerned, they're one and the same," he said smoothly. "I was hoping you'd given some thought to my offer."

"And I was hoping you'd taken me at my word when I told you I'm not selling and never will. It looks like we both have reason to be disappointed."

"The way I figure it, eventually you're going to realize you're wasting your time. No matter how many coats of paint you slap on the place, nobody's going to want to live here."

"Then I guess it's a good thing I plan to do a lot more than paint the place."

"All by yourself? It's an awful big job for one woman. I hear you've had some trouble finding anyone to help you work on the place."

Maggie pinned him with a glare. "Did you hear about my trouble, or did you cause it?"

He made a baleful face. "Now that's not a very nice thing to say."

"And keeping people from working for me isn't a very nice thing to do."

Dalton held up his hands in a helpless gesture. "You can't lay that at my door, Maggie. The house did that all by itself."

She barked out a laugh. "I know this town has

a weird thing about this house, but it's not a living thing."

"It doesn't need to be. You might have spent summers here with your grandparents, but everyone else lived here, and they all know about this house. Nobody wants anything to do with it. It would be best for everybody if you figured that out now."

"My grandfather didn't keep the house all these years just to have it torn down as soon as he was gone. He believed it was worth saving and someday people would live here again."

"You'll have to excuse me for saying so, but your granddad was a fool."

"Now why would I excuse you for saying that?"

His smile couldn't have been more patronizing. "It would be the neighborly thing to do."

"I'm not sure that matters, considering you're not interested in being my neighbor."

"Now, Maggie—"

Whatever response he'd been about to offer was cut off by the sound of footsteps slowly crunching toward them. Maggie immediately lifted her head toward the noise. She couldn't remember the last time she'd been so happy for an interruption.

Then she spotted the man walking toward them and her apprehension returned. This was a small town, and she knew most of the residents, at least in passing. She'd never seen this man before.

He was big, with broad shoulders and long limbs, but also leaner than she might have expected for a man of his size. Beneath a faint dusting of light

stubble, his cheeks were lean to the point of gaunt-
ness. But it was still a nice face, she noticed almost in
spite of herself. He wasn't bad looking by any means,
his features blunt and masculine, his skin fair with
just a touch of the sun. His dark blond hair was thick
and shaggy, more, she suspected, because he didn't
bother cutting it that often than for style reasons. She
could easily imagine it being tucked beneath a cap,
which would certainly fit the regular button-down
work shirt, jeans and scuffed work boots he was
wearing.

As he approached, his eyes met hers. They were
blue, a bright, deep blue, the color rich enough that
she had no trouble recognizing it even from several
feet away. Nor the emotion swimming in them.

Sad, she thought, the strange thought floating
through her mind. He had sad eyes.

It took her a moment to realize who he was. She
didn't recognize his face. In fact, she was certain
she'd never seen him before. Then the shape of his
body sank in, and it hit her that she had seen him
before. Last night.

It was John Samuels.

The realization sent another jolt of surprise
through her. He wasn't anything like she'd imagined.
And she had imagined, during the long stretches of
the night when enough time had passed that she'd
let down her guard slightly and her thoughts had
wandered. She'd pictured someone dark, no doubt
influenced by the way she'd first met him, when he'd
been nothing more than a shadow. This man wasn't

dark, but despite the fairness of his hair and skin, she couldn't quite describe him as light, either. She wasn't sure how to describe him at all.

"Morning," he said, the low rumble of his voice offering additional confirmation.

"Morning," she echoed faintly.

"Everything okay?"

She nodded tersely. "Fine."

He'd come to a stop just behind Dalton, who scowled up at him. She half wondered whether the newcomer's presence alone or the fact that he was significantly taller than the older man was the cause of his irritation. "Who are you?"

The demand in Dalton's tone brought her annoyance back with a vengeance. She could tell John didn't much care for it, either. Eyes narrowing, he hesitated a beat before opening his mouth to answer. That split second was all it took for the impulse to take hold within her. Without even thinking about it, she answered before he could.

"This is my new employee."

Two sets of eyes shot to her, one startled, one appraising. She stared back at the latter, ignoring Dalton. There was no hint of what he thought of her statement, no surprise or relief or happiness. Whatever he was feeling, he was keeping it to himself.

Uncertain how she felt about that, she turned to Dalton. The older man was glaring at John, his face bright red. She didn't know if it was from anger or frustration at being foiled. She didn't really care.

Either way, she liked it and had to do her best not to smirk.

"Dalton," she said, clearly startling him. He jerked his head toward her. She fought a smile. "You'll have to excuse us. We have a lot of work to get to. Thanks for stopping by, though. It's nice to know you're looking out for me."

She couldn't entirely keep the sarcasm from her sickly-sweet tone. From the look he shot her, he hadn't missed it. With a sharp nod, he turned from her, ignoring John, and stomped his way back to his car. She and John watched in silence as he backed out of the driveway and pulled into the street.

Once there, his car paused briefly just behind John's truck. No doubt Dalton was taking note of the license plate. She wouldn't be surprised if he was planning on checking up on her new employee at the first opportunity.

"Does that mean I've got the job?"

The sound of his voice pulled her attention back to his face—and the decision she'd made so rashly. She had to admit that it had largely been spurred by the desire to stick it to Dalton. So much for his claim that she wouldn't be able to find anyone to work on the house. The impotent rage on his face had made it worth it.

Of course, now that he was gone and the moment had passed, she had to face the consequences. She knew nothing about this man beyond the vague suspicion he wasn't being entirely truthful with her. He could be dangerous. He could be a killer. And she would be alone with him for hours on end if she gave him the job. Most days passed without her seeing a single soul.

But rescinding the offer would only make her look like a fool, and give Dalton a satisfaction she in no way wanted to grant him.

"On a trial basis," she said quickly, watching his expression. "That okay with you?"

He shrugged a shoulder. "I don't have a problem with proving myself."

It was the right answer. She liked people who were willing to let their work speak for itself.

Besides, she'd bet anything Dalton was planning on running a background check on her new employee, saving her the trouble of doing it herself. He had enough connections to get it done, certainly more than she had at her disposal. If he found anything shady in the man's past, she had no doubt he'd be back to rub her nose in it as soon as he could.

Of course that wouldn't do her much good if the truck was stolen, or she was already murdered and her new employee ran off to parts unknown by the time the background check came back. But even as she thought it, she found herself dismissing the idea. She had the feeling she was the last person who should be judging anyone's character, but there was just something about him that made her think he wasn't a bad guy. He didn't seem dangerous or creepy or dishonest. He seemed—

Sad, she thought again. He seemed sad.

She felt an uncomfortable pang of recognition in her chest. She watched him tilt his head back and scan the house, those deep blue eyes sweeping over the exterior. The emotion wasn't just in those eyes. It seemed to cling to him like an aura, something weighing heavily on him. And as someone who still had her share of sad days, she could relate.

She did her best to shake off the wave of empathy, definitely not wanting to go there. Whatever was haunting this man wasn't her concern. All that mattered was that he was the right man for the job.

She watched him scrutinize the house. If he wondered why it was in such bad shape, he didn't show it. Suddenly it occurred to her that he probably didn't know the house's history. She didn't doubt that the first person he met in town would waste no time enlightening him. It would be better if she told him herself up front. Despite his claim that he didn't scare easily, she might as well find out for herself. Her big show in front of Dalton would ring awfully hollow if her new employee changed his mind in short order.

"Come on," she said with a jerk of her head. "Let me show you the house. Then you can let me know if you still want the job."

THIS was it.

His insides clenching, Sam watched his new boss head up the steps and took a deep breath before doing the same. Her words and the ominous note in her voice might have given another man pause, making him wonder exactly what it was she was about to reveal that might make him second-guess working for her. Not him. He already knew everything he suspected she was about to tell him. Despite her words, he already knew he wanted the job.

No, it was the very act of setting foot in this house again that made him hesitate. This was all happening too fast, before he was ready. He didn't normally act so quickly and without thinking things through first, having long ago learned the cost of impulsive choices. But it felt like he'd jumped on board a moving train and was being carried away much faster than he'd anticipated or was comfortable with. He'd made the decision to come here on the spur of the moment, getting into the truck and just driving. Then he'd seen that flyer, then he'd come here, then he'd been hired, and now he was about to walk into a house he'd never wanted to see again. It was too fast. He'd barely had time to absorb what was happening.

"You coming?"

He jerked his head to see the woman standing just inside the doorway, a curious and none-too-reassuring expression on her face. The corners of her mouth were turned down as she stared at him. He had the feeling he was blowing this. She looked distinctly wary.

She. That's how fast this was happening. He'd been hired by this woman and he didn't even know her name.

"Sure," he said. "I was just wondering what the polite way was to ask for your name."

She blinked at him, her caution fading into embarrassment. "Oh," she said, "I guess that would be a good place to start, wouldn't it?"

"I could just go with 'Hey, you.'"

A faint smile flickered across her lips. "That won't be necessary. It's Maggie. Maggie Harper."

It was a nice smile—and a fleeting one. Within seconds, it had faded, her mouth forming a thin line.

For the first time, he looked at her, really looked at her. She was an attractive woman, probably in her early to mid-thirties. Her dark blond hair was pulled up in a no-nonsense knot at the back of her head, a few loose wisps hanging around her face. Like him, she was dressed in jeans and a long-sleeved shirt, the clothes fairly worn, the wardrobe of somebody ready to work. Her body had a kind of ropy leanness, the kind earned from activity and labor, and he knew without question that this was a woman who knew how to work and get a job done.

He only hoped she didn't get in the way of the job he had to do.

"Good to meet you, Maggie."

She nodded tightly and turned her back to him, stepping inside. Drawing in one last breath, Sam forced his legs to climb the steps and follow her into the house.

The first thing that struck him was the stillness. Other than the motion and sounds caused by Maggie herself, nothing moved, and the silence was absolute. The entryway opened into a room on either side, both of them almost completely unfurnished. There was a sleeping bag rolled up in the room on the right. Otherwise it was empty. He could see a basic attempt had been made to clean up a little, but it was very much a house where work was in progress. Sunlight poured through the windows, revealing a multitude of dust particles hanging in the air.

In front of him was a steep staircase leading up to the second level. And beside it, a hallway leading back to where the kitchen was. It didn't matter that he couldn't see that room from where he stood. He knew it was there, as a sudden tension gripped him, holding him in place just inside the doorway, unable to do anything but stare in that direction.

His heart began to pound, slamming against his chest wall like it was demanding to get out. The noise rattled through him, filling his ears with the heavy beat. Except he thought he heard something else over it, something distant emerging from the echoing silence of the house to fill his head.

Screaming. Someone was screaming.

Frantic cries. Desperate pleading. Sounds of raw, gut-wrenching agony.

It wasn't just anyone, either.

It was a little kid.

A child was screaming. Crying. Pleading.

Endlessly screaming.

"Are you okay?"

The sound of her voice jolted him into awareness. He glanced over at where Maggie stood in the room to the right. She was frowning again, that same appraising look in her eye.

He didn't let his expression shift in the slightest, even as he swallowed hard and tried to slowly pull in a breath. "Fine," he said shortly. "I guess I didn't figure just how much work this place would need."

"Is that a problem?"

"Not for me. I could use the work. It just seems like most people would save themselves the trouble and tear it down to build something new."

Her face hardened. "Yeah, well, people tend to throw things away too easily."

There was an angry note in her voice, something almost like bitterness. "I take it you like old houses."

"I love them."

"Have you restored one before?"

"More than one. I used to own a restoration business back in California. With my husband," she added after a noticeable pause.

A husband. She wasn't wearing a ring, not that that necessarily meant anything. Someone who worked with her hands as much as this woman had to probably wouldn't bother with one. But something about the way she said it made it clear she no longer had a husband, and the subject wasn't a happy one.

There was a story there. And it was none of his business. He had too many secrets of his own to go poking around in anybody else's. It had nothing to do with why he was here, and that was all that mattered.

"This is a long way from California," he noted, just to fill the silence.

"My grandfather owned this house," she said. "He died last year and left it to me. I decided to come back and fix it up."

"I guess he had a hard time keeping up with the place."

"The last few years he didn't get around as well as he used to," she said with a trace of regret. "And he actually didn't live here, but the place meant a lot to him. He designed it himself and had it built for him and my grandmother. It was their dream home. They'd lived here only a few years when she was injured in a car accident and had to use a wheelchair the rest of her life. This house was no longer suitable for their needs, with all of its stairs, both inside and out. They moved into another house, but my grandfather couldn't bring himself to sell this one. He rented it out for a while."

An image emerged from the recesses of his mind, the face of a man. His first thought was that it was an old man. No, he'd thought the man was old when he'd seen him, but he'd probably only been in his fifties. Ancient to a child, but only a decade or two older than Sam was now.

Maggie sighed. "I might as well tell you now. If you decide to stay, you'll hear it soon enough from just about anyone in town." She drew a breath. "Two people were murdered here. The people my grandfather rented the house to, they were a young family. Two parents, something like three or four kids. One night the parents were murdered here in this house."

Five, he silently corrected. There'd been five kids, though not all of them had been home that night.

He saw she was waiting for his reaction. He simply nodded. "I know."

She started. "You know?"

"A guy at the truck stop told me when I picked up the flyer." It was the truth, not that he'd needed the story.

She sighed deeply, shaking her head. "Of course. I forgot to ask how you knew where to come. I should have known someone had told you, though I would have thought he'd warn you off. I'm a little surprised he gave you directions."

He hadn't. Not that she needed to know that. "Maybe he thought I needed to see the place myself to be scared off."

She eyed him closely. "And the history of the place didn't make you think twice about asking for the job?"

"A lot of places have had bad things happen in them. Doesn't mean there's anything wrong with the place itself."

He had the feeling he'd said exactly the right thing. Both her expression and her posture eased, leaving her looking far more relaxed toward him than he'd seen her in the brief time he'd known her.

"That's what I think, too," she said. "Unfortunately, it's very much the minority opinion around here. Most people just want to see it torn down. That's what that guy was doing here. He's a local builder, Dalton Sterling. He's been offering to buy the property from the moment I came back to town. He wants to tear down the house and build a new one in its place."

Dalton Sterling. The name was familiar, though he hadn't immediately recognized the face. "You didn't like the price he offered?"

"I wouldn't like any price he offered. There's nothing wrong with this house. It doesn't deserve to be thrown away for no reason."

Interesting choice of words. Thrown away. The fierceness, the anger in her words made him eye her closely again.

She'd turned away from him, not looking directly at him. Her jaw was clenched, her face tight with that same anger in her voice.

There's a story there.

None of your business, he reminded himself. *Stick to the reason you came here.*

She glanced up at him. "I guess it's not even worth asking if you already knew all of this before you even came, but do you still want the job?"

"I do."

She nodded. "Then it's settled. Let me show you the rest of the house."

He braced himself for her to move toward the kitchen, somewhere he still wasn't entirely prepared to go. Instead, she moved back to the entryway, to the stairs. His tension eased slightly, allowing a hint of relief to creep in, along with determination.

It was done. He was in. The first step in his hastily formed plan was complete.

Now it was time to get started on the rest.

Chapter Three

"I hear you hired someone to help you with the house."

A few weeks ago, Maggie might have been surprised that her friend Annie had already heard about something that had happened only hours earlier. After several weeks in town, she'd gotten used to just how fast news traveled around here, especially since so much of that news seemed to have involved her.

The someone in question had left for lunch ten minutes earlier. She'd given him twenty bucks to pay for both his lunch and get something for her, as well. Comfortable there was no chance of the conversation being overheard, Maggie put her cell phone on speaker and set it on the kitchen counter so she could focus on scrubbing thirty years' worth of grime from between the counter tiles.

"Dalton didn't waste any time getting the word out."

"From what I hear, he came storming into the diner and threw a fit."

And from there, the news had spread like a virus. At the very least, she had no doubt it had made some people sick.

"I'm sorry I wasn't there to see it. I think I would have enjoyed that." Just remembering how red the man's face had gotten when she'd announced John was her new employee made her lips twitch.

"So who is this guy?" Annie asked.

"He's new in town. Was just passing through when he saw my flyer at the truck stop and decided to check it out."

"You hired a complete stranger? What else do you even know about him?"

"I know that after two weeks he was the only applicant for the job."

"He could be dangerous. He could be a killer, for all you know."

"He gave me a reference. And we worked together all morning and he managed to avoid chopping me up into little pieces so far. That seems like a good sign."

"Talk to me when you get through the afternoon alive."

"And then you'll just worry about tomorrow."

"You better believe it."

Maggie smiled. She had to admit it felt nice to have someone care about her, no matter how unwarranted the concern. She'd been on guard most of the morning, but John had been nothing less than a model employee. He'd followed her instructions, done whatever she'd asked and proven he'd known exactly what he was doing. Whatever else she didn't know about him, he hadn't lied about his experience. She'd watched him closely for even the slightest hint of him looking at her funny. He never had. In fact, he'd barely given her a second glance. Under different circumstances, it would have been quite the blow to her ego. Hell, she wasn't sure it still wasn't.

In the background, she could hear one of Annie's kids—most likely Casey, the youngest—babbling. "Annie, you already have three kids to mother. You don't need to worry about me."

"I can't help it. It would be easier if you'd give up this restoration idea so I didn't have anything to worry about."

"Look, I know you don't approve, even if you are nicer about it than anyone else in this town—"

"It's not that I don't approve." Annie sighed. "I just hate the idea of you wasting all that time and money for no reason."

"It's not for no reason. When I'm done, the house is going to look like a brand-new place."

"Where no one will want to live."

"You don't know that."

"Mags, I've lived here my entire life. It's the Murder House. Believe me, nobody's going to want to live there."

"Don't call it that," Maggie said automatically, unable to keep the faint trace of offense out of her voice. Even as she heard it, she had to acknowledge how ridiculous it was, being offended on behalf of a house.

"It doesn't really matter whether or not I call it that. Everyone else in this town is still going to."

Maggie threw her head back and groaned loudly. "What is the deal with the town and this house?"

"What's the deal with *you* and that house?"

"It's a perfectly fine house. Well-designed. Solidly built." By Dalton himself, she conceded, if only to herself. He'd been the contractor who'd built the house based on her grandfather's designs all those years ago. For that reason, she was somewhat surprised he was so eager to tear it down.

"I think we both know it's not really about the house," Annie said, softly but pointedly.

"Yes, it is," Maggie said immediately, not about to let the comment or the sympathy in Annie's voice get to her. "This is about a perfectly decent house that has no business being torn down just because something bad happened in it a long time ago. It's been almost thirty years. It's time for people to get over it already."

"It's part of living in a town where not much happens. Yesterday's headlines stay in people's minds a lot longer when there's nothing new to replace them. There have only ever been two murders in this town, and they both happened in that house on the same night. It's hard to get past that."

Maggie recognized the tone in Annie's voice and could practically picture her friend shuddering. "I don't remember you being as creeped out by the house or the murders when we were kids."

"Maybe it's because I have kids of my own now

and it's hard not to think about that part of it. Those people had four or five kids, little ones from what I remember. Little kids who were left to wake up and find their parents butchered in the morning. Just the thought of it…" Maggie could hear Annie's voice hitch as her words trailed off.

Maggie suppressed a shudder of her own. She had to admit, it was a chilling thought. Those poor children. She couldn't even imagine what it must have been like for them. She wasn't sure she wanted to.

Almost in spite of herself, she cast an uneasy glance over her shoulder, feeling the echoing emptiness of the house a little too keenly.

"But it's more than that," Annie continued. "Whoever killed them was never caught, you know? No one was ever punished, and nobody even knows why it happened. There's not exactly a lot of turnover in the population around here, which means that if whoever did it is still alive, there's a good chance that person is still living here. Who wants to be reminded that their neighbor could be a murderer?"

No one, Maggie had to admit, even if she couldn't quite say so to Annie.

Annie's words stayed with her long after they ended the call. From the moment she'd decided to restore the house, she'd brushed off any reference to what had happened here, because she hadn't thought it mattered, because it shouldn't. It had been so long ago. People should have been able to get past it.

But maybe Annie was right. Maybe no one could get past it as long as there was no real resolution. No punishment. No explanation for why such a terrible thing had happened at all.

Ignoring it and hoping it would go away may have been the wrong approach. Perhaps what she needed to do was confront it head-on.

Because reasons did matter, she thought as an uncomfortable twinge struck her. They mattered a lot.

She knew that better than anybody.

AFTER leaving the house, Sam drove straight into the heart of Fremont, looking for a restaurant or a diner. It didn't take him long to spot one. This was a small town, and the restaurant was one of only a handful of businesses on the main street, and the only eating establishment.

There were a couple of fast-food places on the outskirts of town, by the highway, that would have been both closer and cheaper, but they wouldn't have suited his purposes. They were too bland, anonymous, places where people didn't linger or make conversation with one another. And it wasn't food he was interested in.

Parking in front of the restaurant, he scanned the rest of the businesses on the street before making his way inside. There was nothing particularly noteworthy that he could see. A police station. A lawyer's office. A grocery store. Only the library grabbed his notice. It couldn't hurt to make a visit there the first chance he got.

Stepping into the restaurant, he saw it was more of a typical small-town diner. A counter ran almost the entire length of one wall. Booths lined two other walls, with tables and chairs arranged in the middle of the room. The place was about half-full, less than he might have expected for a Sunday afternoon.

As soon as he set foot inside, he saw most of the patrons check to see who had entered. Most of the gazes lingered.

He did his best to ignore them. There was no formal host, which seemed fitting for a place like this. Instead, a waitress strode toward him from the other end of the counter as soon as she saw him, excusing herself from the customer she'd been talking to. She was a bottle blonde in her fifties, wearing the usual waitress uniform but no name tag. Probably didn't need one in a place like this.

"Table or booth?" she asked, already reaching for a menu from the holder at the end of the counter.

"Can I get something to go?"

"Sure thing." She placed the menu on the counter and gave it a little pat. "Just let me know what you want."

Sam felt what seemed like every eye in the place on him as he opened the menu. The usual small-town curiosity about a stranger, or something more than that?

He did his best to act like he hadn't noticed their interest as he scanned the menu. Maggie hadn't told him what she wanted, saying anything was fine with her. He didn't care much, either. Figuring he couldn't go wrong with a couple burgers and two orders of fries, he closed the menu and raised his head to call the waitress back.

He didn't have to bother. He looked up to find her standing halfway down the counter, watching him like everybody else. As soon as he glanced up, she was moving again, sauntering toward him. "What can I get you?"

He told her. She didn't bother writing down the order, taking the menu and stepping to a window behind the counter, calling it out to the cook on the other side.

Sam might have liked to try striking up a conversation with the waitress, someone who most likely knew plenty of the people in this town. She didn't come back toward him after putting in his order, even though the menu holder was at his end of the counter. Instead, she moved away to the other end, keeping the menu in her hands, as she went back to talking to the man she'd been speaking with when he entered. She leaned close. Sam didn't miss the glances she sent in his direction.

His nominal business completed, he leaned against the counter and scanned the room with what he hoped looked like idle curiosity. Sure enough, damn near every eye in the place was fixed on him, some doing a better job of hiding it than others. He tried not to make eye contact, even as he scoped out every face for any that seemed familiar. None did at first glance. Then again, it had been a long time. There was no telling if he had a chance of truly recognizing anyone. Even if his memory could be trusted, everyone would look thirty years older.

One of the men seated alone at a booth suddenly tossed his napkin down on the table and rose. Pulling his wallet from his back pocket, he moved to the counter a couple of feet away from Sam, placing his check on the surface. "I'm ready to settle up, Gracie."

"Sure thing, Clay." The waitress took his check and the twenty-dollar bill he'd laid on top of it, then moved to the register a few feet away.

Sam waited. The man had gotten up and come over to stand near him for a reason.

A few seconds later, the man turned and looked at him, his eyes scanning Sam's face with what would have been uncomfortable thoroughness if Sam was the type who was easily unnerved.

Sam stared back, keeping a neutral expression on his face. The man looked to be in his sixties, with thinning gray hair, a paunch and a pinched expression. Something in his face made Sam think he might have been a handsome man once, although his glory days were clearly far behind him.

The man nodded at Sam, the gesture not particularly friendly. "Afternoon."

"Afternoon," Sam returned.

"You new in town?"

"Just got in this morning."

After a beat, the man extended his hand. "Clay Howell."

"John Samuels," he returned, the name coming easier this time than it had the first.

Sam could see the man turning the name over in his mind, trying to place it, and he saw when he'd failed to. "You been to Fremont before?"

"Can't say that I have."

"Passing through?"

"Actually I just got hired on a restoration project. An old house over on Maple."

The man didn't seem surprised, not that Sam expected him to be. He didn't seem anything, simply nodding, his eyes never leaving Sam's.

"You know two people were killed in that house."

"So I hear."

"That doesn't bother you?"

Sam tried to make it look like he was thinking about it. He shrugged a shoulder. "It's sad, sure, but I hear it happened a long time ago."

"Not long enough for some people."

"Did you know them? The people who were killed?"

Clay Howell's eyes narrowed, the first hint of outright anger appearing in the redness that darkened his cheeks. "I'm not sure that's any of your business."

He'd certainly hit a nerve there. "No offense intended."

"Best not ask questions like that if you don't want to cause offense," the man spat. "You won't make too many friends around here as it is working on that house."

"I'm not here to make friends. Just here to do a job."

The waitress reappeared, setting the man's change on the counter next to him. He took a single bill, leaving the rest there and motioning for her to take it. "See you later, Gracie."

"Later, Clay," the waitress echoed faintly.

Shooting Sam one last glare, the man moved past him toward the door.

"Your order will be right up," the waitress told Sam before heading back to the other end of the counter. From the look on her face, that couldn't happen soon enough for her.

Sam stayed where he was, leaning casually against the counter, and turned the encounter over in his mind. Interesting. Maggie was right. People around here certainly were weird when it came to that house.

If he wasn't mistaken, asking a simple question had just earned him an enemy, his second that day if he counted the man Maggie had pissed off by hiring him.

If that was what asking one question was going to get him, then he was more than prepared for them to be just the first of many.

Chapter Four

The graves lay in a nearly forgotten section of the cemetery. Whoever had chosen their location had likely hoped for exactly that to happen, for the two people buried in the plots and what had happened to them to be forgotten. Most of the surrounding graves were much older, the stones indicating their inhabitants had died more than a century ago. But thirty years earlier, space had been made to fit two more plots into this location where they'd be easily overlooked.

Sam supposed he should be angry, but he hardly had any room to judge. This was the first time he'd been to the cemetery. He'd done as good a job of ignoring these graves as anybody, and he didn't even have plot placement to blame for it.

Dawn had begun to break a short time ago, the thin light of morning illuminating the layer of fog that hung over the graveyard. Somehow, being able to see the fog made it more eerie than when it had been darker. He hadn't expected to stay this long, coming just before dawn in hopes of getting in and out unspotted, not wanting to have to explain to anyone why he was here. But it had taken him a while to find the graves, searching the more recent section of the cemetery first. And once he finally located them, walking away didn't seem so easy to do.

He wondered who'd paid for the plain stones. The flat slabs contained only the occupants' names and the years they'd been born and died. Nothing about their lives. Nothing about their relationship to each other. Nothing about the people who'd loved them or the sadness left in the wake of their loss.

Grief, stark and heavy, welled up from the pit of his stomach, and the back of his eyes began to burn. Words he wanted to say more than anything pushed at the back of his throat, gagging him, begging to be released.

I'm sorry. I'm so sorry...

But whatever remained in these graves, he couldn't fool himself that the people who'd been buried here would hear those words. Or that forgiveness would be so easily granted.

Lost in his thoughts, he heard the crunch of tires on the road behind him too late. Not that he could have done much about it. It wasn't like he could run. Whoever it was had already seen him, seen his truck. There was no use trying to hide.

He turned and saw that a police cruiser had pulled up behind his truck. He bit back a curse. It would be hard enough trying to come up with a plausible explanation for why he was here at this time of day for a regular person. A cop would be twice as suspicious.

A single figure stepped from behind the driver's seat and started through the fog toward him, slowly materializing in the haze. He was a big man, maybe in his early forties. As he'd done with nearly every face he'd encountered so far, Sam tried erasing thirty years from the man before him to see how he must have looked back then. Only people like Maggie Harper, whose age automatically meant they weren't worth considering, had been exempt.

It took him a moment to make the connection. Then it hit him, recognition setting off a chain reaction of emotion inside him. Surprise. Wonder. Brief delight. Then crushing dread.

From the look on the man's face, he had the most reason to feel the last one.

The man came close enough that Sam could really see his face clearly, a familiar face with thirty years of wear on it. "Hey, Sam," he said, the tone and cadence the same despite coming from a voice several octaves lower.

For a second, Sam actually considered lying, before admitting there wasn't much of a point. Doing so would only embarrass them both. "Hey, Nate."

Nate nodded, as though he'd needed that final confirmation. "Been a long time."

"Yes, it has."

"Did you really think no one would recognize you?"

"So far, you're the only one who has."

"That you know of."

It was a fair point. No one else had confronted him with his identity, but that didn't mean they didn't know. Which raised the question of why not if they had. He'd be interested to know the answer.

"I don't think I look much like I used to, do you?"

"No, you don't. I almost didn't recognize you."

"So how did you?"

Nate shrugged a shoulder. "Can't really explain it. You're still you, that's all."

"I'll just have to hope nobody else knew me as well."

"As well as your best friend?"

"Yeah."

Nate shook his head and sighed. "What's going on, Sam? Or is it John? What's with the name?"

"I figured it was better if nobody knew it was me." The truth of his identity would lead to all kinds of uncomfortable questions he'd rather avoid. Or maybe it was the answers that were uncomfortable, each more so than the last.

"Why?" Nate demanded with the kind of insistence Sam would have expected from a cop.

Obviously nonanswers weren't going to get him anywhere, which was why he was better off avoiding questions in the first place. "I thought people might be more willing to open up to me if they didn't know my connection to what happened."

Nate snorted. "You must not have been in too many small towns in the past thirty years if you thought anyone would be more willing to talk to a stranger than a native."

"I can't say that I have."

"So where have you been?"

"All over the place." And no place at all. No place that mattered.

Nate made an impatient noise. "It's been thirty years. Why come back now? Why after all this time?"

There was one of those uncomfortable questions, with an uncomfortable answer. He swallowed hard. "I need to know the truth. It's time."

"Long past time, I'd say."

"Can't argue with you there."

"So what took you so long?"

"I had my reasons."

A trace of sympathy entered Nate's eyes, the sentiment shining past the impatience, and Sam had to look away. Nate probably thought he knew what those reasons were, but even he didn't know the true weight of the guilt Sam had carried all these years.

He buried his hands in his pockets. "Anybody else been here?" he said as casually as he could.

Nate didn't need clarification as to whom he meant. "Nope. You're the first."

It wasn't the answer he'd expected—or wanted. He'd figured most, if not all, of the others would have been back before now, at least once in thirty years. He'd hoped Nate might know something and he realized just how hungry he was for information. But none of them had come back. Because they had busy lives, or because they wanted to forget, like he had, even if they didn't have nearly as much reason? Either way, he probably wasn't entitled to that information, even if Nate did have it.

Sam glanced at the man's uniform. "I don't remember you wanting to be a cop."

"I didn't. Not until that night."

Of course. He should have known. That night had affected a lot of people besides him.

"Did you ever tell anybody what happened that night?" Nate asked.

"No."

"I looked at the file myself a few times. Not much there."

Sam couldn't keep his interest off his face. "Can I see it?"

"I'm pretty sure that kind of thing's against regulations."

"That's not what I asked."

Nate stared at him for a long moment before lowering his gaze and nodding tersely. "I'll see what I can do."

"Thank you," he said, meaning it more than those two words could begin to express.

"I'll leave you alone, but you might not want to stay too long. No telling who else might show up next."

"Thanks."

"Good to see you, Sam."

"You, too," he said, swallowing hard against the sudden thickness in his throat. And it was, so much so that it surprised him. As he watched Nate move away into the fog, he tried to think of a single person he'd known in the past thirty years who'd been as close of a friend to him as this man had once been. There hadn't been, of course. He hadn't—couldn't—let there be, not the same way, not when he had too many secrets to keep. They'd only been boys, but boys who went everywhere together, boys who talked about everything with each other. Nate had practically been another brother. Another brother he'd turned his back on.

And now he was a man, damn near middle-aged, the same as Sam. Nate was probably married. Probably had kids and a mortgage and a thousand other things in his life Sam knew nothing about. Strange to think how little he knew about someone he'd once known as well as himself.

"Nate."

Almost to the car, the other man stopped, then slowly looked back.

"Are you going to tell anybody who I am? That I'm not a stranger?"

Nate didn't answer for a moment. Sam couldn't read his expression, but he felt Nate's gaze wash over his face, as though searching for something.

"It's been thirty years, Sam. I'm pretty sure that's exactly what you are."

MAGGIE glanced at the clock on the truck's dashboard, hoping she'd left herself enough time to accomplish what she needed to at the library before it closed. She and John had been busy enough that she hadn't had a chance to make the library run she'd been wanting to since her conversation with Annie yesterday. Not about to let another day pass without getting the information she wanted, she'd left John alone at the house, trusting him enough to leave him on his own for a few hours.

She'd called ahead to find out what time the library closed. From the tone of the woman on the phone, it had been a stupid question. No doubt the hours were common knowledge to the locals. The woman's voice had seemed to convey the message that anyone who didn't already know when the library was open wasn't welcome to visit at any time.

After the last few weeks in Fremont, she was used to feeling unwelcome, Maggie thought. By now, the idea barely fazed her.

As she passed through the quiet streets, she took in her surroundings. Fremont wasn't a very big town, and much of it was familiar to her. At the same time, it was odd how different the place seemed from what she remembered. She'd never felt unwelcome when she'd been here as a child. But then, she'd never really gone anywhere without one or both of her grandparents back then. Even though the townspeople may have disapproved of her grandfather's stubborn insistence on keeping the house, he was still one of them. And as his granddaughter, she had been one of them, too.

And now she wasn't.

It really was as simple as that. From the moment

she'd made her intentions clear, people she remembered, people who clearly remembered her, had
treated her far differently than they had before. Arms
that had once been open were now folded shut. Backs
were turned resolutely against her.

A hard lump formed in her throat. She did her best
to swallow it. After everything that had happened in
the past year, she'd hoped to retreat into the sheltering
comfort of a place she remembered so fondly. But it
appeared a person really couldn't re-create the past.

The library was a squat one-story building toward
the end of Main Street. Spotting it up ahead, Maggie
pulled into a parking space in front and climbed out
of her truck.

She was about to turn and head into the library
when a sudden chill slid through her, raising the
hair at the back of her neck. She hesitated, instantly
recognizing the sensation.

She was being watched.

Without moving her head, she slowly scanned
Fremont's small downtown area. There was no one
obviously in view. That just left all of the windows
on the buildings lining the street. The late-afternoon
sunlight shone down upon the glass, turning them
into mirrors and making it impossible to see who
was on the other side.

Any one of the windows could be hiding an unseen
watcher.

Or all of them might be.

The sensation was so overwhelming that it was
entirely too easy to believe. That every impenetrable

window hid a watcher, like the entire town was staring at her, waiting for the slightest sign of weakness, wanting her to fail.

And they did. The eyes watching her weren't just observing emotionlessly. They were angry. Hateful. She tried to convince herself she was imagining things, but couldn't manage it. The feeling was too strong.

Pure malevolence.

Doing her best not to let her unease show, she raised her chin and squared her shoulders before slowly turning and entering the library.

Her tension didn't ease once she was inside. A woman stood at a counter in front of the entrance. As soon as she looked up and caught sight of Maggie, her expression hardened, her frown tightening so firmly into place that it was almost impossible to believe her lips were capable of doing anything else.

It took Maggie a few seconds to recognize her. It wasn't just the many years since Maggie had last seen her, though they were evident enough in every line and wrinkle on the woman's face. No, it was her expression. Shelley Markham had been the librarian here when Maggie had been a child, and Maggie had never seen her look at her—or anyone else— with anything but a smile. Just another indication of Maggie's changed status around here.

Maggie tried to force a smile of her own, something that proved a challenge to maintain the longer she met Shelley Markham's unsmiling visage.

"Hi, Mrs. Markham. I don't know if you remember me. I'm Maggie Harper. I used to come here—"

"I remember you," the woman cut her off, her tone making it sound as if it wasn't a good thing.

Maggie kept her smile as unmoving as Mrs. Markham's heavy frown. "I'm sure you've heard I'm renovating my grandfather's old house on Maple. I was hoping to look up some old newspaper articles about the Ross murders." There was no point in trying to put it more delicately.

She never would have thought it possible, but the woman's frown actually deepened. "Didn't that man who works for you find what you were looking for?"

Confusion made Maggie lose her grip on her smile. "I'm sorry?"

"That man working for you. He was here a few hours ago looking up stories about the murders and printing them out."

Maggie stared at the woman blankly. A few hours ago... This had to be where John had come during his lunch break. She hadn't asked him to bring her anything, but she'd assumed he'd gone back to the diner, or maybe one of the fast-food places on the outskirts of town.

Instead he'd been here, looking up stories about the murders.

Why?

The woman's eyes narrowed to slits. "You did know he was here, didn't you?" Her tone seemed to indicate she suspected the answer was no, and added an unspoken "you idiot" to the question.

She didn't have to say it. Maggie felt it as keenly

as if she had. The information the woman provided had ensured that. She was the one who'd hired the man. She was the reason he was in town, and now he was running around doing things she knew nothing about, giving the impression they were under her orders, or at least with her knowledge.

And she had no idea what he was up to—or why.

Another man doing God knows what behind her back.

You idiot, she heard in her head, and it definitely wasn't Shelley Markham's voice doing the talking.

Anger surged from her gut, and every instinct screamed for her to race to her truck and storm back to the house to ask John what the hell he was doing.

Which was exactly what she couldn't do, of course. She wouldn't give Shelley Markham and all the people she'd be on the phone with the moment Maggie stepped out the door the satisfaction of knowing what a fool she was.

She had enough people who knew that. Once was enough for one lifetime.

She slowly drew in a deep, silent breath. With some effort, she regained her smile. "Of course I did. As a matter of fact, he didn't find what I was looking for, so I came to search for myself." She chuckled, the noise sounding forced to her ears. "If you want something done right, you have to do it yourself, right?"

The woman simply pursed her mouth and turned

away without a word, leaving Maggie to follow her to the files of microfilm and the viewing machine.

And for the next hour, Maggie forced herself to sit there under the force of Shelley Markham's unrelenting stare, printing every single story on the murder that came up on the screen without really reading them.

When all she could think about was the man she'd invited into her life, and wonder what other secrets he was keeping from her.

MAGGIE bolted from the truck, flinging the driver's side door behind her and stalking toward the house. Her anger hadn't subsided in the least on the drive back. If anything, it had only grown the more time she'd had to stew over the situation.

Stomping up the front steps, she threw the door open. "John?" she called.

No response.

The front rooms were empty. Only the echo of her voice interrupted the stillness.

She heard nothing to indicate he was upstairs. Moving through the kitchen to the back door, she spotted motion in the backyard. Pushing through the door, she started to call his name again.

Then she saw him.

The word died on her tongue, every thought in her head vanishing in an instant.

He was standing in the backyard, which had been tall with grass and choked with weeds when she'd left. The lawn was freshly mown now, the scent of cut grass heavy in the air. He must have found the old lawnmower in the back shed her grandfather had used in the days he was trying to keep up with the place, tending to the yards to keep the house presentable for occupants who would never come.

But that wasn't what grabbed her interest—and held it so tightly her eyes seemed locked into place.

John was raking the lawn clippings into a bag.

He was also bare to the waist.

Perspiration left a fine sheen over his face and torso, so he practically seemed to glisten in the late-day sunlight. The golden rays fell upon his body, illuminating every hard ridge and defined muscle, and there were certainly plenty of both. She watched helplessly, knowing her mouth had fallen open slightly and unable to do a thing about it, as he moved, the muscles shifting, tensing, with every motion.

As she'd seen even when he was fully clothed, he was lean, perhaps too much so for a man with his large build. Somehow it worked on him. The lack of bulk simply left a physique that was perfectly formed, his pecs packed and tight, his belly flat, both dusted with a thin layer of dark blond hair. There was a tattoo on his right bicep, some kind of military insignia that made her think he must have served in a branch of the armed forces. The faint line of hair trailed down from his belly button into the waistline of his pants, the worn jeans hanging dangerously, impossibly low, yet not nearly low enough, the view tempting, tantalizing her with the possibility of what remained stubbornly out of sight.

Her tongue, moving on an instinct all its own, flicked out to moisten her lips, and she suddenly realized her mouth had gone completely dry. She had no trouble understanding the cause, finally recognizing the way her heart was pounding in her chest and an ache had begun to throb low in her belly. It was something she hadn't thought she'd feel so soon again, if ever, and hadn't really wanted to.

Awareness. Desire.

Pure *want*.

Surprise jolted through her, nearly overpowering the rest. It wasn't like she'd never seen a man's bare chest before, or a man working without a shirt on, sweat drenching his body.

But she'd never seen this man. And somehow, in a way she couldn't explain and wasn't sure she wanted to, that seemed to make all the difference in the world.

Then he turned, putting his back to her.

The flash of libido was instantly forgotten, replaced by shock.

Scars, deep and thick, crisscrossed the whole of his back. These ridges were no less hard than the ones she'd admired on his front, although the heat of desire in her belly had died at the sight of them. She could barely see the muscles in his back shifting through the web of them. There was no way scars like that could have been caused by a single incident.

No, they would have been inflicted over time. And the pain they must have caused… She could only recoil in horror at the idea of what must have been done to this man.

Before she could control the response, she sucked in a breath, the gasp coming out entirely too loud and painfully clear.

She clamped her mouth shut, but it was too late. The sound seemed to hang in the air, echoing endlessly in her ears.

John froze, his spine stiffening, then slowly glanced back at her. Almost immediately, he lowered his gaze. Not a flicker of emotion passed over his face, and she had no idea what he was thinking. He turned, facing her again. Embarrassment heating her cheeks, she didn't so much as peek at that incredible view again, keeping her eyes on his face. He stepped over toward the lawn mower she now saw resting a few feet away and reached for the shirt hanging off the handle, quickly shoving his arms into it.

"I'm sorry," she said. "That was rude."

"My fault," he replied roughly, not sounding the slightest bit as embarrassed as she was. "I kind of forget they're even there anymore. Should have kept my shirt on anyway."

"What happened?"

He shrugged a shoulder, not looking at her. "It was a long time ago."

"While you were in the military?" He glanced at her. "Your tattoo," she said.

He grunted. "Something like that."

It wasn't exactly an answer. The curious—okay, nosy—part of her wanted to press the point, but it really wasn't any of her business. She'd already been rude enough as it was.

"Sorry," he said again. "I didn't think you'd be back so soon."

The reminder of her early return brought back the cause of it, along with her irritation. The source of the scars wasn't the only secret he was keeping from her, and the others certainly were her business. "I didn't think I would, either. I was going to spend the afternoon at the library doing some research."

She saw him pause in the act of tugging his shirt over his belly. "Find anything interesting?"

"Besides the fact that you were there over your lunch break doing the exact same thing?"

He finally looked at her, his expression still unreadable. "Is that a problem?" he asked simply, without the slightest bit of chagrin or challenge in his voice.

Hell, yes, she wanted to say. "It's a mystery, and I have enough of those as it is."

"Since I've gotten to town, I've gotten the cold shoulder from everybody I've met except for you. Either this is the most unfriendly town in the country, or everybody has a problem with me working for you on this house. I wanted to know why."

"I told you why. People were murdered here."

"Yeah, thirty years ago. That's a long time for people to be bothered by it, isn't it?"

"It's a small town. People have long memories,

especially when not much new happens to replace the past in their minds."

He started toward her, stopping a few feet from the bottom of the steps. "Then maybe I ought to know a little bit more about it. I'm guessing that's why you were there, too."

She ignored the comment, not about to admit he was right. "Why didn't you just ask me?"

"Honestly, it didn't seem like something you wanted to talk about."

Okay, he had her there. "You still should have told me you were interested," she said stubbornly.

"I'm sorry. I didn't know it would bother you. Is there a reason you don't want me reading up on what happened here?"

"It's not that." She sighed. "But as I told you—and you've already seen for yourself—people aren't too happy with me and my plans for this house. The fact that you're running around town doing things I don't know anything about won't exactly make me look any better in anyone's eyes. You should have seen the way the librarian looked at me when she thought I didn't know you'd been there."

"If it was anything like the way she looked at me, she probably looked like she'd spent the day sucking on lemons."

In spite of herself, Maggie had to chuckle at the accuracy of the image. "You've got that right."

"Then I am sorry," he said. "I never meant to cause you any trouble."

The sincerity in his voice was unmistakable.

Staring into his serious expression, she believed him. Regardless of the end result, he really hadn't meant to cause her trouble. And considering how few people could say the same at the moment, she couldn't help but be affected by the words.

Uncomfortable with the sudden, pathetic wave of gratitude that washed over her, Maggie cleared her throat. "So what did you find out?"

"Not much. I didn't really have any time to read any of the news stories. I just printed out as many as I could and thought I'd read them tonight."

"Is that really what you want to do with your free time?"

"What else am I going to do? It's a small town. I don't really know anybody else and nobody seems interested in getting to know me. What about you? Find what you were looking for?"

She fought the urge to fidget. "I, uh, made some copies of my own. I didn't really get a chance to look at them at the library."

The gleam that entered his eyes told her he recognized she'd planned to do the same thing she'd just tried to talk him out of. To his credit, he didn't bring up her hypocrisy. "Okay, so why don't we go over those stories?"

Her eyes flared in surprise. "Together?"

"Sure," he said, as if it was the most logical thing in the world. "It'll be getting dark soon and I figure we'll be calling it quits for the day, right? No point in doing it separately if we're going to be doing the same thing. Besides, maybe one of us found something the other didn't."

He was right, of course. If they planned to spend the evening doing the same thing, there was no reason not to do it together.

Even so, she hesitated. He was her employee, and she wasn't entirely sure she was comfortable with the idea of socializing with him beyond normal working hours in any way. She needed him too much to risk his getting the wrong idea.

Then again, she was the one who'd been struck speechless by the sight of his bare chest. Remembering her reaction to it, the echo of which rumbled through her at the memory, maybe he wasn't the one she had to worry about getting the wrong idea.

But it was more than that, she thought as a wary feeling nagged at the back of her mind. Yes, what he said made sense. Everything he had did on the surface. He had an explanation for everything, just as he had from the moment she'd confronted him in the middle of the night. Yet as it had that night, she couldn't escape the feeling that something wasn't quite right with the situation, that there was far more the man wasn't telling her.

She tried to convince herself she was being overly suspicious. She wanted to believe she was. Because he was just about the only friendly face she had in this town. And he was here and he was once again offering his help, and she needed somebody who was on her side.

And the idea of sitting alone in the house as the

darkness gathered, reading stories about the murders all by herself, wasn't exactly appealing.

Even as she thought it, she noticed the shadows falling heavily across the back lawn and realized just how dark it had gotten. Dusk was descending, and rather quickly from the looks of it. Before long, it would be pitch-black out here.

And she would be in the house. Alone.

"All right," she said, before she could think better of it. "Let's see what we both found."

He nodded and pointed behind him with his thumb. "I'll put the mower away and get my copies out of my truck."

"We can do it in the kitchen." They would have to. It was the only room in the house with a table and chairs.

For a moment, something passed over his features. A hint of his own misgivings, perhaps? Though she couldn't imagine why he would have any. It had been his idea.

"Sounds good," he said so smoothly she wondered if she'd imagined what she'd seen.

She didn't respond, simply watching him move back to the mower. She wasn't entirely certain she agreed that this was a good idea, as that uneasy feeling continued to nag at her. But it was too late. She couldn't change her mind now without looking like a fool.

She could only go through with it and hope she hadn't made a mistake.

Chapter Five

Sam shifted uneasily in his chair, unable to shake his discomfort. What he wouldn't give to be anywhere else. He should have thought the idea through better before he'd proposed it. Naturally, Maggie would have wanted to go over the articles here, rather than in a restaurant or some other public location where they'd fall under open scrutiny. And he couldn't exactly invite her back to his motel room without it coming across all wrong. Of course it had to be the house.

So here he was, not just in the house, but in this damned kitchen, after dark.

Night had fallen quickly, the darkness thick and impenetrable. The lights in the kitchen turned the windows into mirrors, reflecting the room back in at him. It was as though there was nowhere he could look to forget where he was, the house—this room— surrounding him that thoroughly.

His hands reflexively tightened on the printouts he'd gotten from his truck, crinkling the paper. He forced his fingers to ease up before Maggie noticed or commented.

No, there was one place he could look, one person he could look at. But the sight of her did nothing to ease his tension.

Maggie's head was bowed slightly as she concentrated on the articles in front of her, sorting through them and spreading them out on the tabletop. Watching her work, he couldn't help feeling a twinge of guilt he hadn't before now. He'd come to her under false pretenses, given her a fake name, gone around town under the cover of working for her while acting behind her back. But this, unlike everything else he'd done, felt like he was using her. Sitting across from her, pretending to help her when he was only helping himself, it finally seemed as though he'd crossed the line.

He should have tried to talk her out of looking into this, convinced her there was no point. He didn't want her involved in this. She'd already caused enough trouble for herself just by trying to restore the house. If there was any chance the killer was still in town, asking questions could bring about an entirely different kind of threat. He had no problem with what that might mean for him, but he'd meant what he said. He really hadn't meant to cause her any trouble.

Even as he thought it, he knew it wouldn't have done any good. He'd known her for only a couple days, but it was enough to tell him she wasn't going to be convinced not to do something when she had her mind set. Her stubbornness regarding the house was proof enough of that.

Besides, he had no intention of stopping, and there was no way he could stop her from asking questions while continuing to do so himself.

Which meant he had to make sure nothing happened to her.

But then, that was what he'd always intended. To make sure no one was ever hurt again because of him.

"Okay," Maggie said finally without glancing up. "I think I've read everything I have. Do you see anything you have that I don't?"

"I don't think so," Sam said. As far as he could tell, he and Maggie had copied all the same articles.

"Do you want to compare notes?"

"Sure," he said, not about to admit he'd barely been able to concentrate on the words in front of him. "What do you have?"

"So, the people who were murdered here—their names were Greg and Emily Ross," Maggie said. "She was a teacher at the local high school. A history teacher, I think I read in one of these. And this is interesting—he worked for none other than Dalton Sterling."

"That guy you were arguing with yesterday?" He'd thought the name had been familiar, if not the face.

"One and the same."

"Did he mention that Ross worked for him?"

"Not a word. I wonder if it's something he was

trying to hide or he just assumed it was common knowledge and I already knew. Maybe I should ask him," she said grimly, sounding as if she had every intention of doing just that.

Sam thought he would like to have a word with the man himself. He wondered if there was any way he could invite himself to that meeting, or if doing so would be too odd. The last thing he needed was to raise her suspicions when he'd just calmed them.

Before he could decide, Maggie continued. "So the murders took place on a Thursday night—"

"Or early Friday morning," Sam corrected without thinking.

He braced himself for her reaction, only to see her nod in agreement. "Right. They happened sometime during the night, most likely within the few hours before dawn Friday morning. Both victims were stabbed to death. Emily was found in the kitchen—" She stopped abruptly, eyes widening, and he watched her realize what he already knew. "*This* kitchen."

She turned and slowly scanned the room, perhaps searching for a telltale bloodstain on the hardwood floors.

He didn't follow her gaze. He didn't need to. He could have pointed it out to her. He'd gone straight to it the first time she'd ever left him alone in this room, unable to avoid it no matter how badly he wanted to.

It was right in front of the kitchen sink. The spot was faded, and anyone who didn't know someone had died in this room might have assumed it was just the normal coloring of that particular piece of wood. Even Maggie herself might not guess that dark splotch marked the place where Emily Ross had drawn her last breath, while her middle child begged her not to die, screaming for help that would never come.

Sam stared straight ahead, fighting the shudder that threatened to quake through him at the images flickering through his mind. It didn't matter that Maggie wasn't looking at him. If he lost even that slightest grip on his control, he didn't know what he might do, might say, after that.

Instead, it was Maggie who shuddered as she slowly turned back around.

She cleared her throat and continued reading. "Greg was found upstairs in their bed. I wonder if that means that Greg was the target and Emily had simply been in the wrong place when the killer entered the house. If Emily had been the target, the killer would have left after murdering her."

"I didn't see anything about Emily being killed first."

"Neither did I. It was just a guess. I imagine they were killed too closely to each other time-wise to tell who was killed first, but none of these articles give details like that. We'd probably need to see the police report for that, and I doubt the local police would just let us see it."

"Right," he agreed, squelching another twinge of guilt. He'd called the police station during his lunch break and made plans to meet with Nate later that night to pick up the file. Even thirty years later, his friend was coming through for him.

He couldn't tell her, of course, but he almost wished he could. Wished he didn't have to lie to her.

But it was too late. He had no choice.

"They had five children, all boys," Maggie continued. "The oldest wasn't home that night—he was staying at a friend's house—but the rest all were. None of them saw or heard anything, and none of them was harmed. They slept through the whole thing. They woke up and found their parents stabbed to death." Swallowing hard, she shook her head. "Those poor kids. They must have been so scared."

"They were."

She glanced up at him. It took him a moment to realize he'd said it aloud, those low, hoarse words filled with entirely too much feeling coming from his own mouth. Hell, just as he'd thought. He was getting too caught up in this, losing control.

Meeting her eyes without blinking, he shrugged. "Like you said, they would have to have been."

"I'm sure. The youngest was just five. The oldest, the one who wasn't home, was twelve, with the others somewhere in between." Frowning, she shook her head again. "It's so sad," she murmured.

He looked at her with eyebrows raised. "You didn't think so before?"

"I didn't really think about it at all. I knew what had happened, but I never really thought about the people involved." She winced. "That probably sounds terrible."

"Not really. Most people don't like thinking about unhappy things. That's probably one of the reasons why the people around here would just as soon see the place torn down. They don't like having to think about what happened here."

"I know you're right, but it's not the house's fault. It doesn't deserve to be torn down just because of what happened here."

"It's just a house. I don't think its feelings are going to be hurt if it's torn down."

"But it's not right," she insisted. "This house isn't like the prefab, cookie-cutter houses you tend to see built today, nothing more than a box intended to match every other box around it. It was crafted with care, built to last and designed to be something special—a home, a place for happy memories to be made and people to live out their lives. It never even had that chance."

Her passion for the subject resounded in every word. "If that's how you feel, I see why you make a living restoring old houses."

"My grandfather used to tell me the same thing, said I was meant for it because houses spoke to me." She smiled. "And I guess that all began with this house. I still remember the first time I saw it. I was six years old, and it was the first summer I came to visit my grandparents. My mother never wanted to come back—said it took her long enough to get out of this town and she never wanted to waste any more time here—and my grandparents had little interest in traveling, even if it had been easier for my grandmother. This was home to them. So the only time I ever saw them was the one month each summer I spent with them. And one day my grandfather brought me here to see the house he built for my grandmother. We stood out front and I thought it was the most beautiful house I'd ever seen."

Her smile turned rueful. "Needless to say, it was in far better shape in those days. It had already been unoccupied for a few years, but he was still taking care of it and it hadn't had a chance to fall too badly into disrepair yet. I asked him who lived here, and he said nobody. I didn't understand how that could be, how such a beautiful house could be empty, so I asked him why. He said, 'Something sad happened here, and now nobody wants to live here.' And I looked at the house and said, 'And now the house is sad.' I don't know why I said it. I just knew it was true. I remember the way he looked at me, almost with approval, like I got it. And I did. I still do."

She cast an eye around the room again. "Don't get me wrong, I know the house isn't really alive, but the feeling is still there. You feel it, too, don't you? The sadness in this house?"

A chill rolled down his spine at both her words and the intensity in her eyes. Yes, he thought. He did feel it. The emotion hung in the air like a thick scent, filling his lungs and choking his senses. It was one reason he'd been glad for the chance to get outside and work in the backyard while she'd been gone. He just hadn't thought anyone else who hadn't been a part of what had happened here would recognize it, too.

He shrugged. "It's just a house," he said, and did his best to suppress the now-familiar pang of guilt at the disappointment that briefly flickered across her face. "Besides, if you're right and there's sadness here, maybe the house deserves to be put out of its misery."

"Or maybe it just needs a fresh start," she retorted, the sudden sharpness in her tone telling him he'd hit a nerve. "A second chance."

"Some things you don't get over," he said quietly. "If you're right, then this house has seen things people don't get over in a lifetime, and there's not going to be any changing that."

Regretting the words as soon as he said them, he lowered his eyes. He felt her watching him and suspected he'd revealed too much again. He quickly scanned the papers in front of him, scrambling for anything that might divert her attention. "Anyway, it's a good thing the kids slept through it, or they could have been hurt, too."

He felt her eyes on him a few more seconds before she finally looked away. "True. That would have been even more of a tragedy. Although now that I know the facts, it does seem strange."

"What do you mean?"

"The killer was able to get into the house and kill two people, and none of the four children heard anything? I guess I always assumed the parents were murdered in their sleep, which would explain why no one heard a sound. They didn't get a chance to fight back or make any noise. Now, that might be true for Greg Ross, but Emily Ross was downstairs and no doubt awake. Didn't she scream or fight back?"

"It could be she didn't get a chance," he said roughly. "The killer could have sneaked up on her."

"Which raises the question of how the killer got into the house. I've seen several mentions that there were no signs of forced entry. That's one of the mysteries about that night, how the killer got in. This may be a small town, but even around here and even back then, they knew to lock their doors at night. When I read that she was downstairs, I thought maybe Emily Ross let the killer in. Maybe she heard a knock and came down. But if the knock was loud enough to get her out of bed, wouldn't one of the kids have heard? And wouldn't her husband have gotten up with her? I have to think most husbands would get up to check who it was rather than let their wives go downstairs alone if they heard someone knocking loudly enough to wake them in the middle of the night."

He tried to ignore the furious buzzing in his ears, tried to choke back the bile he felt at her words, at the images they raised.

At the truth he could never admit.

He forced himself to speak, even though he nearly choked on every word. Anything to keep her from looking at him and seeing the emotion he was convinced was written on his face. "You're right. It is strange."

She continued as if he hadn't spoken. "Of course, there's the possibility that she happened to be up, which is why she was awake to let someone in. It seems far-fetched, though. Not to mention, in that case, there surely would have been some noise for someone to hear, either an argument or a scream because she would have seen the attack coming, especially since it says she was stabbed in the chest and stomach. If that's what happened, it's hard to believe that not only four children, but Greg Ross, as well, slept through the whole thing."

"Not if she didn't have time to scream," Sam said, the words sounding so far away it was as if someone else was saying them. "Not if she had her back turned when the killer came after her and she turned around at the last moment right before she was stabbed."

"That's true. And she probably wouldn't have felt comfortable turning her back on someone she didn't trust. Heck, she wouldn't have let someone she didn't trust in the house in the middle of the night at all. Which would make the killer someone she considered a friend." Maggie let out a slow breath. "I can see why the townspeople don't like thinking about it. Not exactly a comforting idea, is it?"

"No," Sam agreed. It wasn't a comforting idea. It also wasn't a correct one.

He couldn't tell Maggie that she was wasting her breath. The idea that Emily Ross had let her killer in might be the best explanation if you didn't know all the facts.

If you didn't know she hadn't had to.

The roar in his ears was so overpowering he had to struggle to make out her next words.

"Of course it most likely had to be someone they considered a friend, because as far as I can tell they didn't have any enemies."

"Obviously they had at least one."

"One nobody, even the victims themselves, seemed to know about. I'm sure you saw that no one was ever charged, and it looks like only one person was even questioned. According to this, Emily had a heated confrontation with a parent of one of her students the weekend before the murder, a Paul Winslow. Evidently it took place at some kind of fair in the center of town. They exchanged words, and Greg Ross had to step in."

"Not exactly a motive for murder."

"No, though I guess it depends on what kind of person this Paul Winslow was, or is if he's still around. Still, that's about it when it comes to people with motive, at least as far as what was reported in the local paper."

"Which means we're not any more likely to figure out who had a motive thirty years later."

"Not from these at any rate," she said, tossing the papers in her hand onto the tabletop with the rest. "It would help if we could talk to someone who was around back then, someone familiar with the people involved."

"Too bad I have a feeling nobody's going to be willing to talk about it."

Maggie thought for a moment. "I can talk to my friend Annie's mom. Irene's lived here her entire life, so she must have been around at the time of the murders and know all about them. She and her husband were friends with my grandparents—that's how I got to know Annie. I'm sure she'll talk to me. I suspect she's the only person who will."

Did he know this Irene? "Sounds like a good idea." Again, he wondered if he could invite himself to that meeting. Maggie might tell him what the woman said, but he wanted to hear it for himself.

He didn't get a chance to say anything before Maggie nodded decisively. "I'll give her a call tomorrow and find out if she can see me. Maybe you can get started on that work we discussed in the upstairs bedrooms while I'm gone."

"Great," he said, forcing enthusiasm in his tone. "I'd be interested to hear what she has to say."

If she got the hint, she didn't respond to it. She'd already returned her attention to the articles, picking up another stack to start reading again.

He fought the frustration climbing inside him. Of course, as far as she was concerned there was no reason for him to come along. This was her mystery. She was the one with the investment in it. He was just a curious bystander, one who'd been hired to do a job and needed to be doing that during working hours.

She didn't know he had far more reason to care

about what had happened here than she did. And there was no one to blame for that lack of knowledge but himself.

Again, the guilt swelled at the secrets he was keeping, the lies he'd told this woman.

He barely felt it. Their conversation had cut far too close, reminding him of just how much he had to feel guilty for.

Nothing he'd done to Maggie Harper could begin to compare to that.

Chapter Six

Maggie stepped beneath the shower's stinging spray and closed her eyes, an involuntary sigh easing from her lungs as the hot water hit her body. The first thing she'd done when she moved into the house was make sure one of the bathrooms was usable. The house's plumbing could use some upgrades, but was in surprisingly decent shape. She'd never been more grateful for that fact than she was at this moment, as the water fell over her, washing away the grime and stress and all the unanswered questions of the day.

She'd stayed in the kitchen for several more hours after John finally left, going over the articles again to see if there was anything she'd missed. She suspected there simply wasn't enough in them for her to miss anything, but didn't want to take the chance. She knew she'd been distracted when she'd read them earlier.

Because John had been sitting across from her. Even when she hadn't been looking at him, even when they hadn't been speaking, she'd never been able to forget that for a minute.

A shudder rolled through her. This time, there was far less pleasure in the sigh that emerged from her throat. She tried to shake off the thought of him, much as she had from the moment he'd finally left. Never mind the unexpected—and unwelcome—return of her libido and her undeniable awareness of him. The man was a mystery, and as she'd told him earlier, she already had enough of those.

Some things you don't get over.

Both the words and the bleakness in his eyes when he'd said them continued to stay with her, raising more questions about the man.

Making her think about things she didn't want to, either.

She'd wanted to dispute his words. She couldn't. She was too afraid she was entirely too familiar with some of those things herself.

She stayed in the blessed sanctuary of the shower until the water began to turn cold, then finally turned off the faucet and stepped out. Almost as soon as she did, the weariness hit her. It was already after midnight. Late, or early, depending on what she decided to do the rest of the night. She'd spent another nearly sleepless night yesterday, again waiting for signs of trouble that had never arrived. She wasn't sure she could do it again. At the same time, she didn't want to risk letting her guard down at the wrong time.

Tonight, though, she may not have a choice, she thought as she stifled a yawn. Every motion seemed impossibly slow as she dried off and pulled on her T-shirt, sweatpants and a thick pair of socks, her sluggish mind forcing her to concentrate harder to accomplish those basic tasks. It felt like she'd be lucky to stay awake ten more minutes, let alone the entire night.

Maybe it wasn't such a bad thing. Basic exhaustion might be the only thing that let her get any sleep at all now that she knew the details of what exactly had happened in this house.

Despite the moist heat fogging the bathroom, she shivered.

Almost immediately, she shrugged off the feeling. It didn't matter. It changed nothing. She wasn't about to start getting as weird about this house as the townspeople.

Still, she lingered in the bathroom, taking her time drying her hair and brushing her teeth.

When she was finally done, she flipped off the bathroom light and opened the door.

And stared into darkness.

She froze, her tiredness immediately forgotten, her senses instantly alert. She could see nothing, not in the bathroom where she'd just turned off the light, nor in the hallway in front of her.

Where the lights should be on.

She knew they should. She'd left them on when she went into the bathroom.

Instead there was only a blackness so absolute she could see nothing at all.

She knew the power wasn't out. The electricity had been working just fine in the bathroom moments before. And she wasn't foolish enough to think all the hallway lights just happened to have burned out at the same time.

No, someone had shut them off.

Someone was in the house.

This was it. The moment she'd been waiting for. The chance to catch any intruders, or scare them off at the very least.

But now that the moment was here, she found herself paralyzed, uncertain what to do as a sudden terror gripped her throat, choking off the angry words she should be uttering. Because this wasn't what she'd expected. She'd expected to be ready, she'd expected to be the one catching someone else off-guard, she'd expected to have the reassuring weight of the baseball bat in her hands, not nothing at all.

She'd expected to scare someone else, not be scared herself.

And no matter how much she didn't want to be, she was.

She tried to think, tried to formulate a plan, with greater and greater desperation, her thoughts frantic.

Whoever was out there would have known she was in the bathroom, of course. Would know that she'd opened the door. Would know that she was standing there now.

Would guess that she'd figured out she wasn't alone.

She wanted nothing more than to turn on the

light, to have that reassuring glow and be able to see something, anything.

Caution held her in place. Because as reassuring as that light would be, she suspected she wouldn't be able to see the thing she wanted to the most. Whoever was out there would be sure of that.

But they would be able to see her.

What would they do? What were their intentions? Just to scare her, or something worse? She might be unarmed. That didn't mean they were.

The sudden squeal was so loud, so unexpected, she nearly jumped. As it was, she barely choked back a gasp. It took her brain a few seconds to get past the shock and identify the sound.

A footstep on a squeaky floorboard.

Right in the corridor in front of her.

Her heart leapt into her throat.

Someone wasn't just in the house. Someone was *right here,* just outside the doorway, mere feet— maybe inches—away. Maybe all she had to do was reach out to grab them. She started to raise her arm to do just that—

Maybe all they had to do was reach out to grab *her.*

She froze again, listening with almost-painful attentiveness, desperate for any clue how far away the intruder was. Another step, another sound. She leaned closer and did everything she could not to make a sound herself. She tried to slow her heartbeat so she could hear above it, tried to breathe slowly and silently.

And listened.

And then she heard it.

The sound was soft and uneven, so low it took her a moment to realize that it was anything at all. Then it took her another moment to realize exactly what it was.

Breathing.

Whoever was out there was close enough that she could hear them breathing.

There didn't seem to be any attempt to make sure she heard the sound, as though they were trying to frighten her with it. They didn't seem to be doing anything but standing there, waiting to see what she would do next.

She immediately knew what that was, cold resolve settling inside her. She wasn't going to cower in the dark. She wasn't going to throw the bathroom door shut and hide until morning. She was going to do exactly what they didn't think she would.

She was going to fight back.

"I know you're out there," she said, the words coming out before she even thought about it, surprising her almost as much as she hoped they scared the intruder. "Who are you? What do you want? Or are you too much of a coward to tell me?"

She listened to her voice echoing down the corridor, the words sounding far tougher than they'd felt.

And waited.

At first there was nothing. She didn't even hear the breathing anymore, the silence so absolute she felt a flicker of uncertainty that she ever heard it at all.

She opened her mouth to throw out another challenge, to try to provoke a response—

"Get. Out."

The declaration floated out of the darkness, the raw fury in it washing over her like a foul-smelling breeze, making her recoil and leaving her skin feeling soiled and unclean. The words were hushed, the tone so low-pitched it was barely more than a whisper. But there was no mistaking the rage in them, the dangerous edge that threatened far more than those words could communicate.

The instinctive fear lasted for only a second, the sensation finally stoking her own anger. The idea that some coward thought they could break into her house and threaten her— The fury finally erupted past the fear, filling her senses and her entire body until she felt nothing else.

"The hell I will," she spat.

The words were barely out when she burst out of the bathroom. Almost simultaneously she heard footsteps heading back down the hallway.

No way. They weren't getting away that easily.

She tore down the hallway after them, ready to give chase, already reaching out to grab the railing before she made it to the stairs, preparing to plunge down them after the intruder.

At the last possible second, intuition broke through the adrenaline, and she realized something wasn't right.

Something that should be there wasn't. Something. But what was it? What—

Footsteps, she registered just before she launched herself down the stairs. There were no footsteps on the stairs.

If the intruder was racing down them, she should be hearing feet pounding down the stairs, the echo unmistakable in the entryway.

But she didn't. There was only silence.

Which meant—

Her own feet had already started to stumble to a stop on their own, instinct causing her to turn—

She never made it.

Two unseen hands came out of the dark, open palms landing firmly and forcefully against her back.

And shoved. Hard.

The scream burst out of her mouth, the feel of it raw in her throat, the sound impossibly far away. Because by the time it came out, she was already falling, tumbling far from where the sound emerged.

She grabbed for the railing, clawing for anything to catch to stop her fall. Her fingers came away empty. Her legs flew out from under her, her entire body seeming to hang suspended in midair. Almost as abruptly, a jolt rocked her body, stars exploding behind her eyes, pain erupting in her backside and down her legs as the lower part of her body hit the stairs and started thudding down them. Her hand slammed against something, then something else, then again. The rails in the banister, she recognized faintly, clawing desperately for one, anything to hold on to as she tumbled backward down the stairs.

It happened so suddenly she didn't realize it had at first. Her fumbling fingers managed to catch something and grabbed hold by pure instinct. Her shoulder wrenched painfully, her arm feeling on the verge of being pulled from the socket. Still, her progress slowed.

Through it all, she finally did hear it, the footsteps she should have earlier, along with the gust of wind as the intruder rushed by.

She reached out with her free arm, grasping for a leg, a hint of cloth, anything she could grab on to to prevent the intruder from getting away.

A leg came flying out of the dark, a foot landing directly in her ribs with unerring precision. She screamed again as pain exploded in her side, her body skidding farther down the steps. Her shoulder pulled, straining agonizingly, nearly causing her to lose her hold on the railing.

She managed to tighten her grip and hold fast, until she was sprawled out painfully on the stairs.

Through the pounding of her heart and her labored breathing she heard the footsteps rounding the corner at the bottom of the stairs and heading down the back hallway.

No. They weren't going to get away.

She forced herself up, unable to restrain the groan that erupted as every part of her body reacted in protest, and plunged down the stairs, leaning on the railing far more than she would have liked.

Kitchen. The intruder had headed toward the back, to the kitchen.

And the back door.

Limping, hurting, she did her best to follow, swallowing the cries of pain that threatened with every movement.

She heard the back door slam against the wall, the glass rattling in the window as it bounced off the surface.

She tried to move faster, each step seeming excruciatingly slow, each one inflicting its own punishment.

The light switch was just inside the entryway for the kitchen. She reached out for it before she got there, already suspecting it would be too late.

The light flared on at her touch. The room was empty. The door gaped open, the hole in the window and glass on the floor indicating how the intruder had broken in.

She gave herself no time to process the scene, lunging to the back door, then through it. The wind immediately slapped her in the face, the gust of it whipping her hair behind her. Wincing against the onslaught, she tore down the steps, her eyes seeking out every inch of the backyard for any sign of where the intruder had gone. Through the back into the trees? Around the corner to the front? Through the shrubs next door?

She saw nothing, no one. The moonlight shone upon an empty yard. Each second that passed without her spotting anything kicked her desperation up another notch. The intruder couldn't have disappeared so easily. It wasn't possible. There had to be something. If not back here, then maybe she should go around the front. She started to turn—

Suddenly a figure loomed in front of her, huge and frightening.

She skidded to a halt, shock making her throat seize up, stifling the scream that rose in it.

Two hands grabbed her shoulders before she could react. The moon was behind him, blinding her, blocking out his face.

"Maggie, what's wrong?"

That voice. It took her a moment to place it, for recognition to push past the shock, the adrenaline, the terror, racing through her.

John. It was John.

Relief slowly seeped into her system. Breathless, she tried to respond but couldn't.

He shook her gently. "Maggie?"

She swallowed, the action seeming impossibly hard. "Someone was in the house," she managed to choke out. "Was it you?"

"No. I was in my truck. I came when I heard you scream."

"Stairs," she groaned, her throat too dry and raw to get the words out easily. "Pushed me down the stairs."

His grip tightened on her arm. "Are you okay?" he asked, his voice deep with concern.

"Fine," she forced out. "Did you see him?"

"No, I was heading for the front door when I heard sounds back here and came around."

The strangeness of his presence finally broke through all the jumbled thoughts racing through her mind. She peered up at him, wishing she could see his face. "What are you even doing here?"

"I wanted to keep an eye on the place. After the trouble you've already had, I wondered if people hearing about us going around looking up stories on the murders might stir up some more."

Again, the answer seemed right—and somehow not. With everything muddled in her head, she couldn't even begin to process the feeling. "Did you see anybody?"

"No. Whoever it was must have approached the house from behind."

"Not that seeing you out front would have stopped him. If having me inside wasn't enough to keep him out, then seeing you out there wasn't going to stop him."

"You keep saying 'he.' You're sure it was a man?"

Maggie hadn't even considered what she was saying, the words coming out on their own. Her thoughts seemed to be racing too fast for any of them to gain traction. She took a deep breath and tried to sort through the muddled impressions. That low, angry voice… It could have been a man, but it didn't have to have been. The hoarse whisper could have belonged to a woman just as well as a man.

She shook her head. "No. I don't know. I didn't

see who it was. I only heard a voice, and it was too hushed to tell if it belonged to a man or a woman."

"What did it say?"

At the memory of those words, she trembled again. "'Get out,'" she whispered. "It said, 'Get out.'"

He said nothing for a moment, perhaps letting the words sink in. "Did you say anything back?"

A faint smile pulled at her mouth. "I said, 'The hell I will.'"

He chuckled lightly. "Good for you."

"Except then he—or she—shoved me down the stairs, kicked me in the ribs and got away clean. I'm pretty sure that makes him—or her—the winner of this round."

"Kicked you in the ribs—" He swore softly, the anger in his voice surprising her. "We need to get you to a doctor."

She waved a hand. "It's not that bad. I don't need a doctor."

"Well, we have to call the cops at least. You need to report this."

"It's a waste of time. We didn't see anything, I'm sure nobody else saw anything, and I doubt the intruder left any clues behind, given how careful they've been in the past. The police will just come out, take a few notes if I'm lucky and nothing will come of it. That's what happened the first few times someone vandalized the house. Eventually I stopped calling."

"This is different. This was assault. You need to put it on the record."

"Don't you get it?" she asked, her voice sounding perilously close to breaking. "It doesn't matter. Nobody will do anything. Nobody cares. I'm on my own here." An uneven breath wheezed from her lungs, hitching as it left her throat. "Nobody cares."

The weariness hit her again, all at once, but this time it went beyond physical exhaustion and everything that had happened that day. Instead she felt the weight of everything that had happened since she'd set foot in this town bearing down on her. The truth of the words was too much to deny. She really was alone in this. She'd just never felt it as much as she did in that moment. She could have been grievously harmed, and with the exceptions of Annie and maybe her mother, no one in this town would care less. She wouldn't be surprised if they threw a parade in the intruder's honor.

To her horror, she felt the first hint of tears prick the back of her eyes, a sob climbing her throat. She lowered her head to keep him from seeing her expression as she tried to regain control. She had a feeling he saw it anyway.

"I care," he said softly.

She nodded without looking up, not taking the comment for anything more than the rote assurance it no doubt was. What else could he say? "I'm sure you do. If anything happens to me, you might not get paid. In fact, I wouldn't blame you if you wanted to be paid daily from now on just in case."

She waited for him to deny it. She waited for

him to tell her that she needed to drop this, that she needed to give up, that it was just a house and certainly wasn't worth risking her life over.

He didn't say any of those things. Before she realized what was happening, he reached down and hooked her chin with his forefinger and lifted her head until she was looking up at him.

"I care," he said roughly. His voice was serious enough that all her thoughts fled, leaving the words and the tone in which they were spoken to sink past her defenses and straight through to her core.

She still couldn't see his face. The moon was behind him, rendering him nothing more than a shadow, just like the first time they'd met. That didn't stop her from peering up at him, trying to read exactly what was in his face as he stared down at her in the dark.

He slowly rubbed his hands over her upper arms, the gesture as comforting as it was no doubt intended to be. It took a moment for the heat generated by the motion to sink past the cold numbness gripping her body, for her to truly feel the impact of his fingers through the T-shirt's thin short sleeves. His hands were large, his fingers blunt and rough against her soft skin. They were the fingers of a man who worked with his hands. Her husband's fingers had felt like that, she acknowledged, even as part of her recognized that in a more fundamental way Kevin's hands had felt nothing like this at all.

In a flash, the same awareness she'd felt when she'd seen him working in the yard and when she'd sat across from him in the kitchen that night came back, pounding through her body, stronger than ever. It didn't matter that she couldn't see him. She felt it just the same, felt his closeness, felt the sound of his voice still rumbling through her. It was far more elemental than a response to his physical appearance, and far harder to deny.

She didn't even try. She simply stood there and let the feeling sink in, felt it build inside her. She finally realized just how close they were standing. And yet, she wanted to lean closer, to step fully into his arms and feel the muscles of his body pressed against her and the heat of him surrounding her. She wanted him to wrap his arms around her and hold her close in a way no one had in a very long time.

As though compelled by her thoughts, he moved closer, his fingers still sliding up and down her arms. She tilted her head back farther, keeping her eyes where his should be. The clouds must have shifted, because the moonlight briefly played across his features, those fleeting glimpses somehow making him even more mysterious. Because they revealed his expression to her, however momentarily, the look on his face both unreadable and intense, his eyes focused on hers. That look kicked her heartbeat up another notch, sent the pressure building within her higher and higher. And she knew, instinctively, with absolute certainty, that he was going to kiss her.

Knew she wanted it, wanted this man more than she had wanted anything in so very long.

Once again, as though caused just by her thinking it, he slowly began to lower his head.

At the last, most dangerous moment, just when that want was about to be fulfilled, reality broke through. She planted a hand against the firm wall of his chest and stepped back, lowering her head and giving it a vigorous shake.

"This is wrong," she murmured, barely able to keep a tremor from her voice. "You work for me."

"You haven't paid me yet."

"And paying you after this would raise the question of exactly what I was paying you for."

He let out a low breath. Though he didn't say anything, she sensed him concede the point.

"Come on," he said roughly. "Let's get you inside and make sure you're okay."

"I'm fine," she said. "I'll be okay. I'm sure he—or she—won't be back tonight. You can go."

"I'm not going anywhere."

She lifted her head in surprise. "What?"

"You shouldn't be alone, especially if you won't go to a doctor. Your injuries could be worse than you think. Besides, you can't be sure that person won't be back tonight. I'm sure you didn't expect them to break in and attack you, either."

"No," she admitted weakly. Things had never gotten so personal before. She hadn't really thought they ever would.

That feeling she'd had in town, that sense of pure malevolence being directed at her, came back to her. Combined with the voice she'd heard tonight, it was hard to deny this wasn't just about the house. This had become about her.

Somebody out there hated her that much. She'd never had that feeling before, and she suspected she couldn't rule out anything a person like that might do.

"Do you think it's a coincidence this happened on the same day both of us were at the library, looking up stories about the murders?" he continued relentlessly. "How long do you think it took the librarian to get that news out?"

"Not long," she agreed, recalling Shelley Markham's pinched face.

"Are you planning on dropping this? Because if not, it's only going to get a lot worse. This isn't just a matter of people not liking the fact that you're restoring this house. Somebody doesn't like the fact that you're asking questions. They came after you personally, and until you drop all of this, they're not going to stop."

He wasn't telling her anything she didn't already know. "Are you trying to talk me into quitting?" she demanded, her hackles rising.

"Would it do me any good?"

"No."

"I didn't think so. You're still planning on talking to this Irene woman tomorrow?"

"Yes." Now more than ever.

"Then I'm going with you."

She frowned. "That's not necessary."

"Yes, it is. I want to get to the bottom of this just as badly as you do."

"Why?"

There was a noticeable beat before he answered. "Like you said, I haven't been paid yet and I need this job. I have a vested interest in making sure nothing happens to you."

Yes, she had said that. But hearing the words coming from his mouth, she didn't believe them. Things had gone past that, become far too personal for her to think this was simply a matter of getting paid. Would he have tried to kiss her if this was just about a job? Maybe he would have. Maybe he was that kind of man. But she didn't think so. She just didn't know what kind of man he was.

I care, she heard in the recesses of her mind. The question was, why did he really? But she doubted he would admit the answer.

Suddenly, a gust of wind smacked her in the face, breaking into her thoughts and making her wince. It finally sank in exactly where they were and how absurd it was to be having this conversation outside in the middle of the night. She glanced around, taking in the shadows filling the yard, all the dark impenetrable spaces that could be hiding anything or anyone. She couldn't hold back another shiver. She started to wrap her arms around herself, only to cringe as she lifted them and a pain shot down her side where the intruder had kicked her.

The terror of those moments came back in a flash. Combined with the uneasiness she felt standing out here in the dark, surrounded by shadows, she couldn't deny that she didn't really want to be alone in the house.

"Fine," she muttered. "Let's just go inside."

She tried to tell herself she just didn't want to argue anymore, that she simply didn't have the energy, that she was too tired. That was why she'd capitulated.

But as he fell into step behind her and she felt his solid presence there, she couldn't help but admit that the feeling most dominant within her was relief.

Chapter Seven

Sam had expected an argument from Maggie once she'd gotten some sleep and last night's events weren't as fresh in her mind. He'd prepared himself for the face-off, ready to go another round with her as soon as she got up that morning. It had been a fight he'd intended to win.

He'd won, but only by default. She hadn't said a word in disagreement. Offering only a brisk morning greeting, she'd called her friend Annie's mother and asked if she was available that morning. The only argument had been over whether she should drive, and since she knew where they were going and he didn't, he quickly let her have her way.

As they passed through town, Sam glanced at her out of the corner of his eye. She stared straight at the road, her face composed, her expression neutral. She hadn't said anything about what had happened last night, had dismissed his question about how she was feeling. The way she was acting, it was as if none of last night's events had happened at all.

He wished he could brush them aside as easily.

Instead, the memories remained all too vivid in his head. The terror of those moments after he heard her scream and thought he'd be too late to help her. The relief when he'd come across her and found she was safe. The fury when she'd revealed what had happened.

The way she'd looked in the moonlight, her face tilted up toward his, her mouth soft and willing, her unbound breasts clearly outlined beneath the well-worn T-shirt she'd had on, her nipples pebbled against the chill.

Swallowing hard, he glanced away. Going there was a bad idea. Just like kissing her would have been.

But damned if he hadn't wanted to. Damned if a large part of him didn't wish he had.

He didn't know where the impulse had come from. She was attractive, sure. He'd known that from the first moment he'd seen her. But it had only been at that moment that something he'd instinctively known had been building between them had finally burst to the surface.

He wanted this woman.

Thank God she'd displayed the control he'd lacked. A personal relationship was a complication neither of them needed, him especially. He had other things to focus on, things he had to do, plans from which he couldn't be distracted. He knew it.

But knowing it hadn't stopped him from spending most of the sleepless night thinking about how she'd looked in the moonlight and what it would have been like to taste her mouth.

Didn't stop him from thinking about it still.

"This is it," Maggie said, thankfully interrupting his thoughts as she made a turn onto another street. "Irene's house is just up ahead."

He cleared his throat. "How do you know this woman again?"

"She and her husband were neighbors of my grandparents, and her daughter was my best friend in town whenever I was here."

"So your grandparents lived on this street?" he asked, surveying it through the window. He wasn't as familiar with this neighborhood as the one where her house was located.

"Yes. This is where they moved when they left the house on Maple. That's their house right there. My grandfather left it to my mother. She sold it right away."

He looked at the house she'd gestured toward as they slowly passed by. It was a solid one-story, ranch-style house on a good-sized lot. Out front, the flowers were still in full bloom. It was smaller than the house on Maple, but more appealing in a way, more comfortable, more like a home, although the comparison probably wasn't a fair one. "Looks like a nice place." Actually, the whole street looked nice, like a real neighborhood, not just a collection of houses that happened to be on the same road, like it was on Maple.

"It is," Maggie agreed. "I wasn't surprised she

managed to sell it so quickly. She didn't even have to come back to deal with it. Not that I think she would have."

"Were they happy there? Your grandparents?"

She seemed to consider the question, a faint smile passing across her face as she remembered. "Yes. I think they were."

"So maybe having to move out of the house on Maple wasn't such a loss for them."

The smile died abruptly as she clearly got his point. She shot him a glare. He looked back, unrepentant. If he hadn't understood her fixation with that house before, he certainly didn't now. If her grandparents had been happy where they ended up, then they truly hadn't lost much by not being able to live in that house.

"You don't understand," she said.

"You're right," he returned. "I don't."

Maggie exhaled slowly, clearly seething. "Here we are," she said shortly. She turned into the driveway of a house several doors down from the ones where her grandparents used to live. Like theirs, it was a large one-story home with a big yard. As they parked, Sam thought he detected the curtains shifting slightly in the front window and suspected their arrival had been noticed.

They didn't speak as they climbed out of the truck and walked to the front door, Maggie's irritation obvious in the stiffness of her posture. Only when the door suddenly opened before they even reached it did she finally relax, though he suspected it took some effort.

A woman in her seventies stood in the doorway, the wide smile on her face aimed directly at Maggie. "Maggie Harper. Aren't you a sight for sore eyes? Come in, come in." She stepped aside and motioned them in.

"Irene," Maggie said warmly. "It's been a long time."

"Too long," Irene reprimanded sternly as she closed the door behind them. "You've been in town weeks now and this is the first I've seen you."

"I'm sorry," Maggie said. "I've just been swamped with the house."

"So I've heard," Irene said, her eyebrows going up. She didn't sound displeased exactly, but there was something pointed in the words.

"I'm sure you have," Maggie replied with a soft sigh. "I hope you're not opposed to me fixing up the house like so many people around here. Even Annie seems to have her doubts."

Irene's expression softened with apology. "I think it's a beautiful house," she said carefully. "But also one with a very sad history. Annie told me about your plans, and I'm afraid I have to agree with her. No matter how much hard work you put into it, there aren't many people who will want to buy it."

"That's what we were hoping to talk with you about." She started. "Oh, I'm sorry. Irene, this is John Samuels. He's helping me with the house."

The woman finally turned her full attention to

him. With gray hair and a round face that matched her plump figure, she looked every inch the kindly grandmother. She surveyed his face, a polite smile firmly in place, her expression revealing nothing. "Nice to meet you, John. That must mean you're not afraid of a challenge."

"Definitely not," he returned. He scanned her face, seeking some sense of familiarity. He found none. If he'd ever met this woman, she hadn't made enough of an impression to stay in his memory.

"Then I suppose you and Maggie are well-suited for one another." She waved them into a living room to the left of the entryway. "Come in, both of you. Have a seat."

The three of them moved into a spacious living room. It was the type of room where everything had its place and nothing was out of it, more a showplace to entertain guests than an actual living space. Irene sat in a chair facing the door, Maggie falling onto the couch beside her. Sam took a chair opposite Irene.

"Can I offer you anything?" Irene asked. They both declined politely. "So what is it you were hoping to talk with me about?"

Maggie leaned forward. "We both thought that if we better understood what happened in the house, we might be able to understand the townspeople's reaction to it, and maybe figure out a way to overcome it."

"You mean, you're trying to solve the murders," Irene said bluntly.

Maggie chuckled lightly. "I guess there wasn't much point in trying to put it delicately."

"No, there really wasn't."

"Obviously what happened at the house still bothers a lot of people, otherwise they wouldn't be so opposed to what I'm trying to do. And I think part of that stems from the fact that the case was never resolved. So we thought if we were able to find some kind of resolution, it might help people get over it. But to do that we wanted to speak with someone who might be able to tell us more about the Rosses, someone who was more familiar with the town back then."

"I have lived here my whole life," Irene acknowledged with a nod.

"Did you know Greg and Emily Ross?" Maggie asked.

"It's a small town. Everybody knows everyone else to some degree."

The answer came with a charming smile, but Sam didn't miss the fact that it wasn't really an answer at all.

If Maggie felt the same, she didn't show it. "Do you know if they had any enemies, anyone with a reason to want to hurt them?"

"As far as I know they were well-liked. Emily was a popular teacher at the high school. Greg was a star of the football team when he attended that high school himself, something that still had him plenty of admirers years later. About the only person in town who didn't like him was Clay Howell."

"Clay Howell?" Maggie echoed.

Irene fluttered a hand. "A high school rivalry, and a mostly one-sided one at that. They were in the same year together all through school and Clay was the quarterback of the high school football team their junior and senior years. You would think that would make him the big shot, but everybody knew Greg Ross was the more talented athlete. He was a running back, had college scouts coming to check him out. Can you imagine, here in Fremont? Greg ended up receiving several offers to play college football on a full scholarship. Clay didn't receive any."

"Still, I'm sure he must have gotten over it."

"I wouldn't be so sure about that," Sam said. "I met Clay Howell at the diner in town the other day. From the way he reacted when I mentioned the Rosses and the fact that I was working at the house, he still doesn't like the mention of Greg Ross's name."

"It's amazing how long some people cling to their high school days," Irene said. "Especially in a small town. Half the men who played on that team when they were in high school still show up at games wearing their letterman jackets years later, the old fools. If you can't button the thing over your beer belly, you have no business wearing it as far as I'm concerned." She shook her head. "Of course, in Clay's case, he probably couldn't help but continue to resent Greg, especially after he married Janet."

"Janet?" Maggie asked.

Irene nodded. "Janet Sheridan. She was the head cheerleader, prettiest girl in school, that sort of thing.

The way I heard it, Greg was the one she really wanted, and it was only after she didn't make any headway with him that she turned her attention toward Clay. He went for her. After all, she was the prettiest girl in school, and there does seem to be a certain symmetry, the quarterback and the cheerleader and all. Still, it couldn't have done much for his ego knowing he was her second choice. Years later, Janet went to work as Dalton Sterling's secretary, and I remember hearing Clay wasn't happy about it since Greg worked for him, too."

"If she was so desirable, why wasn't Greg interested?" Sam found himself asking.

"Greg only ever had eyes for Emily, and she for him. Some folks thought they'd break up after she went away to college and he stayed in town, but they didn't."

"Greg didn't go to college?" Maggie asked. "What about his scholarship?"

Irene grimaced. "He was in an accident the summer before he was to leave for college. He was injured, ended up not being able to play anymore. The college withdrew his scholarship. He ended up staying in town and going to work for Dalton. And after Emily graduated, she came back and took a job at the high school. They got married and started having kids right away."

"The five boys," Maggie said.

"Yes. We all imagined one day we'd see those boys out on the field, playing for Fremont High like their daddy. The older ones already looked like they

were going to be as big as their father. But it wasn't
to be."

"What did happen to the boys?" Maggie asked.
"I didn't see anything about it in the paper."

"The state took them away. Neither Greg nor
Emily had any family left to take the boys, and no
one came forward and said they were willing to take
them in."

"Not even one of them?"

"That would have seemed strange, wouldn't it?
Somebody saying they were willing to take one, or
even a few, but not all of them? It would have been
odd to split them up that way. Though I expect they
were split up anyway. Hard to imagine many people
with the resources to take in five children at one time
like that."

"It's so sad," Maggie murmured. "A tragedy on
top of a tragedy."

"Very much so," Irene agreed.

Sam didn't say anything. He couldn't. He could
only sit there, tension gripping his body, and hope
they'd move on.

Maggie finally continued. "In the paper, it said that
Emily Ross had an angry public confrontation with
a Paul Winslow the weekend before the murders."

"No surprise there. Paul Winslow was always
getting into rows with people." She made a tsking
sound. "I'm afraid not much has changed. The man
still has quite a temper."

"Do you know what the argument was about?"

"Of course. Half the town overheard. It was about

his daughter, Teri. She must have been, oh, fifteen years old at the time."

"Was she in one of Emily Ross's classes at the high school?"

"I don't know about that, but I do know she worked as a babysitter for the Rosses, taking care of the youngest boys after school until Greg or Emily could get home from work."

Maggie straightened in her seat. "So she must have had a key to the house."

Irene looked at her strangely. "I imagine so. Why?"

Maggie waved off the question. "No reason. Is that what the argument between Paul Winslow and Emily Ross was about, his daughter's babysitting job?"

"I think it had more to do with Paul not doing a very good job raising his daughter. His wife died when the girl was just five years old, and he was raising her all by himself. She was such a shy girl, pretty but bookish, and he was never much of a father to her. I'm not sure he ever wanted to be. Rumor was that the only reason he and his wife got married was because she was pregnant. As far as I know Teri doesn't even speak to him anymore."

"So he's still in town?"

"Yes, they both are. Teri actually teaches at the high school herself now. Maybe Emily Ross made an impression on her."

"So Teri wasn't just a babysitter, she was close to the Rosses?"

"I think Emily tried to look out for her, let her stay over for dinner most nights since Lord knows if Paul would have bothered making dinner for her. Anyway, that day at the fair, Emily tried to talk to Paul about Teri, probably wanting him to get involved more in his daughter's life. The next thing everybody knew, Paul erupted, the way he always did. He got right into Emily's face, telling her to stay out of his business and not try to tell him how to raise his own daughter." She shook her head. "It got so heated Greg had to step in and tell Paul to back off. Then Greg and Paul got into it. It was quite an ugly scene. Pretty much ruined the fair for everybody that day."

"And less than a week later, Greg and Emily Ross were dead. I can see why he was questioned after the murders."

"Yes, he was really the only suspect, and only because of that incident coming so shortly before the murders."

"But he wasn't charged."

"No. There was no real evidence that he had anything to do with them. Him, or anybody else."

"And thirty years later the case remains unsolved."

"Indeed. So you can see why you're wasting your time, Maggie. Both of you," Irene added, glancing at Sam. Her expression softened with a touch of sympathy. "I understand your frustration with people's reactions, but if no one's managed to solve those murders by now, what makes you think you have any chance of doing so?"

Maggie shook her head and shrugged lightly. Sam didn't hear her answer. He barely managed to bite back his own.

Motivation, he thought darkly. The difference was that he was motivated in a way no one else had been before now, and unlike everyone else, he didn't intend to give up until he had answers.

"I THINK Irene gave us some good places to start," Maggie said as she drove them back to the house.

"Absolutely," John agreed. "What do you want to do first?"

Maggie didn't even have to think about it, having made up her mind as soon as Irene had revealed what she had. "I think we should talk to Teri Winslow."

She sensed John turn and look at her in surprise. "The babysitter? Why?"

"Because I've been thinking about how the killer got into the house. If the killer didn't break in, and Emily Ross didn't let that person in, there's really only one other possibility, especially if it was someone she never would have let in during the night—that the killer had a key. Like maybe a babysitter who picked up the kids and took them home after school while the parents were at work."

He made a noise of disbelief. "You think the babysitter killed them? What's her motive?"

"That's not what I'm saying. You heard Irene. Paul Winslow had a terrible temper, and we know he had an angry confrontation with Emily Ross just days earlier, one where Greg was involved. He could have taken his daughter's key and gotten into the house."

"Even if he did, do you really think he would kill two people over some kind of parent–teacher dispute?"

"I don't know. We don't really know what the dispute was about, or just how bad Paul Winslow's temper was. Maybe that dispute was enough to push him over the edge. I think it's worth looking into."

"I don't," he said bluntly. She flinched at the surprising curtness of his answer, but he didn't seem to notice. "I'd rather talk to Clay Howell. From his reaction the other day, he still doesn't like hearing Greg Ross's name thirty years later. So either he's still harboring enough of a grudge that it was definitely bad enough to kill over thirty years ago, or something else is bothering him, like maybe guilt?"

"Even if he hated Greg Ross, why kill Emily? Irene didn't say anything about any animosity between the two of them."

"It could just be she was in the way. If he came upon her after entering the house, he might have had no choice to keep her from stopping him."

"But how would he have gotten into the house? Surely she wouldn't have let him in."

"I'm sure he could have found a way," he said, his voice plainly dismissive. "Just because the police didn't figure it out doesn't mean there wasn't one. They couldn't figure out who the killer was, but we know there was definitely one of those."

The house loomed up ahead. Maggie pulled up out front. "All right," she said, unable to keep the doubt from her voice. "We can talk to him, too, right after we talk to Teri Winslow."

John shook his head. "There's no point in both of us wasting our time. If we split up, we can cover more ground. You talk to Teri Winslow if you want. I'll track down Howell, and we can compare notes later. I'll meet back up with you later, okay?"

Without waiting for a response—indeed, before she could make a sound—he climbed out of the truck and walked away.

Maggie could only gape after him as he slung himself into his truck and started the engine. Moments later, the vehicle pulled away.

The surprise she felt at his abruptness made sense. The hurt caused by his departure did not.

It was there nonetheless. She swallowed hard, her eyes pinned on the back of his truck as it rapidly disappeared from view.

By now she should have been used to having a man walk away from her.

But somehow, despite that fact and the knowledge that this man in particular owed her nothing, the sight didn't hurt any less.

Chapter Eight

The look in Maggie's eyes when he'd brushed off her idea stuck with Sam long after he left her and made his way back into town. So much for his vow not to hurt her.

But he didn't have time to waste chasing down leads that wouldn't go anywhere, and he knew Teri Winslow and her key were definitely a waste of time.

He just couldn't tell her why.

He pushed the thoughts aside and forced himself to concentrate on tracking down Clay Howell. He could always ask around town where he might be able to find the man, but even if anyone was willing to tell him—and he had strong doubts about that— he didn't want word reaching the man that he was looking for him. The element of surprise would be to his benefit.

Instead, he drove back to the library and, ignoring the sour-faced librarian, checked the local phone book. There was only one Howell listed, not Clay, but someone with the initial J. Janet? If so, strange that the listing would be in her name alone. Regardless, Sam took down the address. Whoever it was, they might know where to find Clay.

J. Howell's address was on the other side of town, close to Irene's. A single car was parked in the driveway. Hoping that was an indication someone was home, Sam parked behind it and walked to the front door.

At first no one responded to his knock. He was about to do so again when the door slowly swung open, revealing a woman in her late fifties to early sixties. Presumably the latter if this was Janet Howell. A brunette with fine features and a trim physique filled out in all the right places, she was still attractive enough to indicate she must have been considered a real beauty in her youth. The only thing marring her looks now was the frown she aimed at Sam, causing her face to settle into angry lines.

"Yes?" she said, her tone distinctly unfriendly, one hand braced on the door.

"Excuse me, ma'am. My name is John Samuels. I'm looking for Clay Howell."

"Clay doesn't live here. What made you think he did?"

"The only Howell listed in the phone book had this address, so I figured I might as well try it. Are you J. Howell?"

"Janet," she admitted with clear reluctance. "I don't think Clay has a landline these days. He mostly uses his cell."

"Then he doesn't live here? I was under the impression you were his wife."

The woman's expression noticeably tightened. "We were married once. We haven't been for a long time."

Interesting. Irene hadn't mentioned it, but maybe she hadn't thought it relevant. "Would you happen to know where I can find him?"

"What's this regarding?"

He considered lying or providing some vague non-answer, but decided it might be more useful to see this woman's reaction to the truth. "It's about Greg and Emily Ross and what happened to them."

The woman's eyes widened a barely perceptible amount, but there was no missing the way she suddenly went pale. All the blood practically drained from her face. "Why would you want to talk to Clay about that?"

"I heard Clay didn't get along with Greg Ross."

"That was a long time ago. High school stuff."

"Really? When I talked to him the other day, it seemed like he still didn't like Greg Ross much."

"If you talked to him the other day, why are you looking for him now?"

"We didn't get a chance to talk that long. I have a few more questions for him."

From the way she started to open her mouth, Sam suspected she wanted to ask what those questions were. Instead, she slammed her mouth shut again. "I'm sorry. I can't help you."

Before Sam could reply, she stepped back and closed the door in his face.

He didn't bother knocking, having no doubt there was little chance the woman would open it again, let alone answer any of his questions.

Still, the encounter had served its purpose, he thought as he moved back to his truck.

Janet Howell knew something. He didn't know whether it was something solely about the Rosses or something about Clay and the Rosses, but it was definitely something. He hadn't failed to notice the way her fingers had tightened on the door, her knuckles going white, when he'd mentioned Greg and Emily Ross. She'd practically been holding on to the door for dear life, as though it were the only thing keeping her on her feet.

Whatever Janet Howell knew, it scared her.

He was still going to talk to Clay Howell. Whether he got anything out of the man remained to be seen.

But somehow he was going to find out what Janet Howell knew.

Something that had her that scared had to be something he needed to know.

MAGGIE figured the best place to find Teri Winslow on a school day would be the high school. It was only twelve-thirty, but Maggie was in no mood to wait until after school to talk to the woman. After John's reaction to her idea, she wanted more than ever to find out if she was right, and she wasn't nearly patient enough to wait until three or four for that to happen. If she was lucky, she might be able to catch the woman during her lunch period.

Driving to the school, she pulled into the visitor parking lot. The high school was a large one-story brick building just to the east of downtown. The main office was directly to the left of the front entrance. A woman standing at a long counter looked up as Maggie entered.

"Can I help you?"

"I hope so. I'm looking for someone I was told is a teacher here, a Teri Winslow." She paused as realization struck. "Actually that's her maiden name. If she's gotten married, I don't know what her married name is."

"It's still Winslow," the woman confirmed. "She's not married. Can I say who's asking?"

"My name is Maggie Harper. It's regarding a personal matter. I was hoping to maybe catch her during lunch."

Maggie suspected she didn't have to explain what that personal matter was. At the mere mention of her name, the woman's eyes narrowed slightly, not enough to be too obvious, but enough to let Maggie know she'd recognized her name.

"She should be on her lunch period right now. Let me see if she's available."

"That would be great." Not entirely comfortable with the woman's eager, appraising stare, Maggie motioned toward the doorway. "I'll wait outside if that's all right."

"Sure," the woman said, a trace of disappointment in her voice.

With a forced smile, Maggie stepped out into the foyer and out of view of the doorway until she didn't feel the woman's stare on her back. Having nothing better to do, she scanned her surroundings. It seemed to be a typical high school entryway. Wooden cabinets with glass doors housed a number of trophies. As she scanned the wall, Maggie's gaze fell upon a metal plaque set among the brick. She automatically moved toward it for a closer look.

IN MEMORY OF
SPENCER BARTON
DEDICATED EDUCATOR, BELOVED TEACHER

Below the words were two years separated by a hyphen, no doubt those of his birth and death. He'd only been thirty-two when he died. Interestingly enough, the year of his death was the year after Greg and Emily Ross were murdered.

She glanced at the surrounding walls to see if there was a corresponding plaque for Emily Ross. She wasn't exactly surprised to find that there wasn't. If there was any kind of memorial for the woman, it must be somewhere else. Somehow Maggie suspected there wasn't one at all.

Whoever Spencer Barton was, he must have died under less scandalous circumstances, enough so that his life was deemed worthy of remembering while Emily Ross's was deliberately forgotten. Maggie couldn't help but feel a touch of anger on Emily Ross's behalf.

"Ms. Harper?"

Maggie turned to find a woman striding down the main corridor toward her. She immediately deduced this must be Teri Winslow. The woman was in her forties, tall and lean, with short brown hair and glasses. There was a no-nonsense quality about her, from her brisk pace to the basic, simple sweater and black slacks she wore to the way she held her head up, her eyes automatically meeting and holding Maggie's. Her lips curved in a polite smile, though Maggie detected little genuine warmth in it.

"I'm Teri Winslow," she said, confirming Maggie's conclusion. "I was told you were asking for me." She didn't offer her hand.

"Yes. Can you spare a few moments?"

"For what exactly, if I may ask?"

"I was hoping to speak with you about your father."

In an instant, the woman's pleasant facade vanished, the bland smile hardening into a grimace. "What's he done now?" she said bluntly.

Startled, Maggie blinked at her. "Nothing that I know of."

The woman didn't relax at the reassurance. "Then what is it?"

"I don't know if you've heard, but I'm restoring an old house on Maple."

"The one you inherited from your grandfather. The Murder House." Her mouth twitched at one corner in what might have been a hint of amusement. "It's a small town, Ms. Harper. Everybody's heard about it. Most of them aren't too happy about it."

"What about you? Are you one of those people?"

Folding her arms over her chest, Teri sighed and seemed to consider the question. "To be honest, I think it would be better for everyone if the house wasn't there anymore. All it does is serve as a reminder of what happened there. I knew Mr. and Mrs. Ross. They were good people. They deserve to rest in peace."

"Maybe they'd rest easier if their killer was caught. That's why I'm here. I admit the reaction I've gotten has made me more curious about what happened at the house. I started reading up about the Rosses and their murders. Your father had an angry confrontation with them a few days before the murders, didn't he?"

"Obviously you know he did or you wouldn't be here asking about it."

"True enough. I was wondering whether you had a key to the house back then?"

"Yes. I used to pick up the younger boys some days after school and walk them home, then stay with them until Mr. or Mrs. Ross got there."

"Is it possible your father took your key?"

"No," Teri said immediately.

The woman's lack of hesitation caught Maggie off-guard. "You sound sure of that."

"I am. I took my responsibility seriously. That key was never out of my possession."

"Really?" Maggie asked, unable to hide her surprise at the certainty in the woman's tone. "I'm not sure anyone can be absolutely positive where everything they have is at any given time. Surely there were some times you weren't holding on to your keys. Maybe you set them aside, or even left them in your purse—"

"And then my father took them and either copied it or used the real thing to enter the Rosses' house? I'm sorry to disappoint you, but it never happened. You're wasting your time, Ms. Harper. My father wasn't even in Fremont at the time of the murders. He was out of town that night."

"Out of town? Where?"

Teri shrugged. "On business somewhere. I'm not sure he ever told me. He just said that morning that he was going out of town and wasn't going to be home that night. And he wasn't, not that night nor the next morning before I left for school. I didn't see him again until the following night."

"He left you home alone?"

"Yes. Not for the first time, nor the last." She smiled thinly. "Now you can see why Mrs. Ross felt compelled to talk to him."

"She must have cared a great deal for you," Maggie said. "Were you close?"

For just a moment, a flash of pain broke through

the woman's calm expression. She winced and briefly glanced away. "She was like a second mother to me. Or a first, since I barely remember my real mother. I spent more dinners at their house than at my own. She certainly defended me like a real mother should." She swallowed. "I wish I'd appreciated it more at the time."

"That must have made your father angry," Maggie said carefully. "Having someone who wasn't family telling him how to raise his daughter."

"It doesn't take much to make my father angry," Teri said. "And yes, he was angry that day, as you've already heard."

"And you're sure he was out of town that particular night?"

Even as she asked the question, she knew it was a foolish one. From her expression, Teri Winslow thought so, too. Likely everyone who'd lived in this town knew where they'd been on the most notorious night in Fremont's history.

"If you don't believe me, feel free to ask around. I'm not exactly on good terms with my father. In fact, I haven't spoken to him in years. No small accomplishment in a town this size, as you can probably imagine. If I thought there was the slightest chance that he was responsible for what happened to Mrs. Ross, I would gladly turn him in myself. Now, was there anything else you wanted to talk to me about?"

"Just one," Maggie said. "Since you were so close

to the Rosses, can you think of who might have wanted to hurt them?"

Teri stared straight ahead, her gaze far away. "No," she said sadly with a tight shake of her head. "I can't think of anyone who would want to hurt them."

The woman's voice rang with honesty, and looking into the bleakness in her eyes, Maggie believed her. Maybe it was wrong putting too much hope in the memories of someone who'd really only been a child at the time, but she was also the only person Maggie knew of who'd been personally close to the Rosses. She didn't know who else might know and had no idea how to go about asking, short of stopping people on the street and literally doing so.

"Okay," Maggie said, swallowing her disappointment. "I guess that was it."

"Good. I should get to class."

Maggie watched Teri Winslow walk away. The woman was certainly convincing. Without any proof otherwise, Maggie was going to have to accept that the killer wasn't Paul Winslow, having gained admittance by using his daughter's key. Which meant however the killer had done it, it was by some other method.

She remembered Sam's vehemence that she was wasting her time, the utter certainty in his voice.

It was almost as if he'd known.

Chapter Nine

Maggie scanned the streets with increasing irritation as she made her way into town late in the afternoon, her eyes seeking a familiar truck that was nowhere to be found. After talking to Teri Winslow, she'd headed back to the house and tried to get some work done, expecting John to show up before long. He hadn't, and her annoyance had grown by the hour. She hoped he wasn't expecting to be paid for today. She'd hired him to work on the house, not run around playing detective.

Especially not without me, a small, petty part of her acknowledged. Then there was the way he'd ditched her in the first place, her initial shock having given way to the anger that continued to simmer in her belly, his mysterious absence only adding fuel to that particular flame.

She'd finally decided to head into town to pick up some supplies she needed—and to figure out where he was.

It was only when she'd pulled onto Main Street proper that she finally saw his truck, coincidentally enough parked just a few doors down from the hardware store. As she climbed out of her truck, she saw John come out of the diner in her direction.

He saw her almost immediately and headed toward her. If he felt any chagrin about his vanishing act, he didn't show it. His face remained as unreadable as ever.

"Where have you been?" Maggie asked point-blank when they were close enough she didn't have to raise her voice for him to hear her—or anyone else could overhear easily.

"Looking for Clay Howell."

"All day?"

"Yep."

"It's a small town. There can't be too many places to hide."

"Apparently he's not in town. He had business of some kind out of town today. Too bad it took all afternoon to get someone to tell me that—or to talk to me at all."

"So it was a waste of an afternoon."

"Not entirely. I talked to his wife—ex-wife, now. She wouldn't talk to me, either, but the way she reacted to the Rosses' names, I had the feeling she knew something."

"Like what?"

"I don't know. I think a return visit is in order."

"By both of us," Maggie said pointedly. "Evidently I need to keep an eye on you."

"Sorry," he said, a faint trace of regret in his voice.

"I didn't think it would take this long and I lost track of the time."

His words carried a ring of truth, and her annoyance eased slightly.

Before she could respond, a voice cut through the air.

"Hey!"

The yell came from behind her, and Maggie didn't react at first, having no reason to believe it was directed at her.

"Hey, you!"

It was closer this time, and Maggie saw John look up and past her. She finally turned and glanced back to see an older man with a shock of white hair, his face red with anger, stalking toward her. Before she could do anything, he was practically on top of her, jabbing a finger in her face.

"I hear you've been asking questions about me."

She blinked at him, nearly stumbling backward to get away from him. "I'm sorry?"

"Well, you damn well should be!"

Taking her by the shoulders, John pulled her back and stepped in front of her. "Is there a problem?"

The man barely spared John a glance. "You're damn straight there's a problem. *She's* the problem. Everybody in town knows that. I just didn't know she was going to come after me!"

"I'm sorry, Mr...." John trailed off, clearly leaving the man to fill in his name. The newcomer didn't take the hint, simply glowering at Maggie. John was forced to continue. "What are you talking about?"

"Why don't you ask her?" he said with another jab of his finger.

"I'm sorry," Maggie said again. "I don't know who you are."

The man barked out a laugh. "That's funny. You don't know who I am, but you don't mind running around trying to accuse me of murder. The name's Winslow. Paul Winslow."

Comprehension pushed past her shock. So this was the infamous Paul Winslow. From the looks of things, his temper hadn't diminished any over the years. Maggie couldn't remember the last time anyone had looked at her with so much fury, if ever. She felt a flicker of relief the man wasn't armed, though part of her suspected that wouldn't have stopped him from starting something if John wasn't standing in front of her. Even now, the man's hands were fisted at his sides, his arms tense and twitching, as though he was barely able to restrain himself from putting them to use.

Maggie pulled in a breath, trying to keep her voice steady as she met the man's stare. "I wasn't accusing you of anything, Mr. Winslow. I was just asking a few questions."

"Asking questions about whether I took my daughter's keys so I could break into that house and hack up those people? Sounds like an accusation to me!"

The school secretary, Maggie realized. She and Teri had been standing outside the office door. The woman must have overheard everything.

"I assure you, I didn't put it like that—"

"Doesn't matter how you put it! Only a damned fool wouldn't know what you meant. Are you calling me a fool now, too?"

"She did no such thing," John said gravely. "We both know that. I was standing right here and heard every word."

"I hear just fine, too," the man spat. "And I know just what she meant!"

"That's enough!"

Teri Winslow suddenly appeared behind her father. She grabbed his right arm and tried to pull him away. "Do you have to make a scene everywhere you go?" she hissed low enough that only her father, Maggie and John should be able to hear.

Paul yanked his arm out of his daughter's grasp. "Stay out of this, little girl. Bad enough I didn't hear about it from you. You weren't even going to tell me at all, were you?"

"Of course not," she said. "What's the point? The last thing you need is a reason to make a fool of yourself."

"'What's the point?'" he scoffed. "A man has the right to defend himself against false accusations!"

Maggie stepped out and tried to assume a soothing tone. "Mr. Winslow, you have no need to defend yourself. Your daughter already told me you couldn't have taken her keys and you were out of town that night."

Winslow blinked at her. "Out of town?" The man frowned in apparent confusion and fell silent for several long moments. "Oh, right. Yes, that's right," he said with increasing assurance. "I *was* out of town that night. So you're wasting your time." He finished on a sneer.

The rapid change in his mood was unmistakable, and Maggie couldn't help eyeing him closely.

Teri made another attempt to take her father's arm. "Fine. Now that that's settled—"

Paul pulled his arm away again and stepped forward, eyes newly ablaze. "If you want to go accusing anybody, you should look at Dalton Sterling. Everybody knows he wants to get his hands on that house of yours. Didn't you ever wonder why?"

Maggie frowned. "He wants to tear it down and build something else on the property."

Paul Winslow laughed. "Of course he does. Probably worried you'll find something wrong with that house."

"What are you talking about?" Maggie was unable to resist asking.

"Oh!" the man feigned amazement, eyes going wide and jaw dropping open. "Nobody told you about that, did they? I guess you really are asking the wrong questions, lady."

"So why don't you tell me what the right questions are?" Maggie said with saccharine sweetness.

"One of Sterling's houses collapsed years ago. Structural problems. Substandard materials. Nearly destroyed his business. They said it wasn't his fault, but who knows if it was true? Who knows if there's not something wrong with that house of yours?

Maybe you should be asking yourself that." His lips curled back over his teeth, pure meanness in his grin.

"Come on," Teri tried again.

He threw his arm up, spinning around to face her. "I'm going, little girl. Don't worry. You won't have to talk to your old man anymore. We both know you don't want to."

Tellingly, Teri didn't deny it. She didn't say anything at all as Paul brushed past her and stomped down the sidewalk away from them.

In the wake of her father's departure, Teri stood stock-still, tense with humiliation. She faced John and Maggie, but didn't meet their eyes. "I'm sorry," she said, barely more than a whisper.

"It's not your fault," Maggie said. "You didn't do anything."

Teri finally looked at her. "Why'd you have to bring all this up again?" she asked bleakly. "Why couldn't you just leave it alone?" Without waiting for a response, she dropped her head, giving it a hard shake, then turned to cross the street, heading in a different direction from her father.

As Maggie watched her go, she finally noticed several others had stopped along both sides of the street and were watching openly.

"Come on," John said, no doubt having seen the interest they'd garnered, as well. "I'll walk you back to your truck."

She hadn't gotten the supplies she'd come for, but as the onlookers continued to simply stand there, watching silently, she suddenly had no interest in staying in the middle of town any longer. With a tight nod, she turned toward her truck.

"Still think Paul Winslow couldn't be the killer?" she muttered under her breath as John fell into step beside her.

"I didn't say that. But you said his daughter told you he couldn't have taken her key."

"And you seemed pretty sure the killer didn't need a key. I guess that keeps him a viable suspect."

John didn't say anything for a moment. "Interesting how he seemed confused when you said he was out of town."

So he'd noticed it, too. "Maybe because he knew he wasn't, which would mean Teri lied to me." She shook her head. "From the looks of things there's no love lost between them, which would indicate she was honest with me about that much. I really didn't think she would lie for him."

"Maybe she didn't. She could have been telling the truth as far as she knew it. Just because he told her he was out of town and she believed him doesn't mean it was true."

"Which raises the question of where he was."

"And what he was doing."

Indeed, Maggie thought with a shudder. She remembered the raw fury in the man's eyes when he'd yelled at her. She could only imagine what Emily Ross had felt like, facing a man like that when he'd been in the prime of his life.

Just as she could only imagine what he was capable of if he'd had a knife clutched in his closed fist.

"IRENE confirmed what Paul Winslow told us," Maggie said, setting her phone down on the kitchen counter. "A couple years after the murders, one of Dalton Sterling's buildings collapsed. Given the time frame, it was a house Greg Ross most likely worked on. It's too late to go to the library, and I doubt any of this made it into the bigger city papers that would be archived online. We'll have to wait until morning if we want to find out more."

"Do you think there's something wrong with this house?" Sam asked, leaning against the doorway.

"Not that I've found. I went over the whole building when I was evaluating what work needed to be done. I would have sworn there's nothing structurally wrong with this building. Maybe I missed something. I might have a better idea what to look for if I knew what was wrong with the other house."

"Well, if there is something wrong with this house, Greg Ross must not have found it, either. He wouldn't have let his children sleep in it if he did."

"But as someone who worked with Dalton, Greg might have known what to look out for. If he'd found something wrong with the other site, Dalton might have been afraid he'd start taking a closer look at the house his family was living in. Or if he did know something was wrong with the other site, that might have been enough for Dalton to need to silence him before he could reveal it to anybody else."

"It's as good a motive as anyone else's," Sam noted.

"Not to mention that, as the person who built the house, there's a chance he could have saved a key, which gives him a way into the house."

Sam grimaced before nodding. "True. There's a chance of that."

Maggie opened her mouth to respond. Any sound she might have uttered was cut off by the noise that erupted at the front of the house, a series of hard thuds in quick succession. The noise was so sudden, so unexpected, it took him a second to recognize it. Someone was pounding on the front door, someone who was none too happy from the sound of it.

They both froze, eyes meeting across the kitchen. Sam arched a brow. "Winslow again?"

"I don't know. Maybe we should call the police."

Before he could respond, a voice called out. "I know you're in there! Open this damn door!"

The voice was vaguely familiar, but not from this afternoon. "That's not Winslow," he said, pushing away from the door frame and turning toward the front of the house.

"Do you know who it is?" Maggie asked, trailing behind him.

"I think so. If I'm right, I didn't need to bother looking for Clay Howell all afternoon. He's decided to come to us."

Howell continued pounding on the door, the blows coming faster and harder by the moment. "Are you sure we should answer it?" Maggie asked, nervousness threading through her words. "The man sounds dangerous."

"Stay here if it'll make you feel safer. I've been wanting to talk to him all day. I'm not going to ignore him now." Especially since he wanted to know exactly why the man was so angry when all Sam had done was try to track him down. Even as he thought it, eagerness made him pick up his pace.

As he'd known she would, Maggie stayed on his tail rather than head back to the safety of the kitchen. Making sure he remained between her and the door, he reached for the knob and pulled it open.

Sure enough, Clay Howell stood on the other side of the door, closed fist raised in midknock. He swayed, struggling to restrain his momentum, clearly not having expected the door to open. He glared up at Sam, wild-eyed, his face red with the same rage that had been apparent in his voice and his pounding.

"You!" he said, opening his fist to poke a finger in Sam's chest. The jab was hard enough that Sam was almost forced to take a step back. He managed to hold his ground. "You stay away from my wife!"

"You mean, your ex-wife?" Sam said calmly, not letting the slightest reaction to the man's fury show on his face.

"She'll always be my wife. You just stay away from her!"

"Who told you I'd been by to see her?" Sam said as though the man hadn't even spoken.

"She did."

Interesting. Evidently the former spouses still felt protective of one another. He couldn't help but wonder why they were no longer married and whether that was relevant.

"Said you were looking for me. I don't know what for, because I've got nothing to say to you."

"In that case, maybe I'll have to talk to Janet again," Sam said, deliberately goading the man.

The man's face flushed an even darker red. For a second, Sam thought Howell was going to take a swing at him. "You even try and I'll press charges for harassment!"

Strange, but the idea that Sam would talk to Janet seemed to bother the man more than Sam wanting to talk to Howell himself. "I'm pretty sure she would have to do that. In fact, if she wants me to stay away from her, she's free to say so herself. I don't know why it's any of your business."

"Because I care about her. She may not still be my wife in the eyes of the law, but like I said, in a way, she'll always be. You upset her, and she doesn't deserve that. She doesn't deserve to get pulled into whatever nonsense the two of you are running around town doing."

"I'm sorry," Sam said, not managing to make it sound any more genuine than he was feeling. "I didn't intend to upset her. I was just looking for you. You're a hard man to track down."

"I'm not here to be at your beck and call, Samuels," Howell sneered. "I don't want anything to do with you at all."

"Why? Do you have something to hide?"

A tic erupted under the man's right eye, betraying the lie he was about to utter. "No."

"Really? Because I hear you and Greg Ross didn't get along."

"Not everybody does. Doesn't mean I wanted anything to happen to him."

"Just the mention of the man's name seemed to bother you when we met at the diner the other day."

"I didn't like you asking questions and stirring up old business everyone would rather forget. I had you pegged. I knew you were trouble from the first time I saw you."

"Or did you know we would figure out you were involved? Is that why you don't want us to talk to Janet? The two of you were married back then, right? So she would know if you did something. Kind of hard to hide it from your wife if you came home in the middle of the night with your clothes all bloody."

"Shows what you know. I wasn't even in Fremont that night. I had to go out of town on business."

Sam couldn't hold back a smirk of disbelief. "Isn't that convenient?"

"Convenient or not, it's the truth. Not that it's any of your damn business. The only thing you need to know is to stay the hell away from Janet. I mean it.

You stay away from her if you know what's good for you."

With that, he spun on his heel and stomped down the steps. Sam watched silently as the man stalked back to his car and peeled out of the driveway with a screech of his tires.

"Boy, we're just making friends all over the place, aren't we?" Maggie murmured as the car disappeared from view. He'd almost forgotten she was even there.

"That's the truth. Hard to believe so many people could be so bothered by a few questions about something that happened so long ago."

"And so mad. I guess Paul Winslow isn't the only one with anger issues."

"They're two of a kind, all right," Sam agreed.

"Isn't it interesting that so many people connected to the case just happened to be out of town that night?"

"Funny coincidence, isn't it? If that's the same story they told back then, the police would have confirmed it."

"Unless there was no way to prove it or disprove it either way," Maggie noted.

She had a point. He still needed to read the case file he had gotten from Nate last night and stashed in his truck. He'd been so focused on Clay Howell all day he hadn't had a chance. And now night was beginning to fall again, he noted, watching the shadows begin to slide across the lawn. Which meant he wouldn't get a chance to anytime soon.

"What do you want to do now?" she asked, and Sam realized he hadn't responded to her previous comment.

He turned to face her. "We get ready for tonight. We already know those two are angry enough to try to pull something. And if someone else is the killer, that person might try something, too, even worse than last night."

Her eyes slid past him toward the lawn, uncertainty flickering in them as she no doubt took in the encroaching darkness just as he had. She nodded. "You're right. Maybe I should order a pizza. It's bound to be a long night."

"Good idea." He watched her head back to the kitchen where she'd left her phone, taking a moment before following. Sucking in a breath, he swallowed his frustration. They'd made good use of the day and gotten no closer to the truth. He hadn't expected this to be easy by any means. If it was, someone would have solved it long ago. But more than anything he wanted answers.

And after all this time, all he had to show for his efforts were more questions.

"WHEN do you want to do another patrol?"

Sam checked his watch, fighting a grimace when he saw the time. He was tempted to say now just to get out of the house, even if wandering around in the dark with their flashlights wasn't much better. "The last one was half an hour ago. Maybe another fifteen minutes?"

He thought he detected a hint of disappointment in Maggie's expression. If that was what she was feeling, she didn't express it aloud. She simply nodded and returned her attention to her notes.

He understood her restlessness. It was only midnight, but it already felt as if they'd been trapped in the house for days rather than hours. The darkness surrounding them was absolute. The sense of danger grew more ominous the longer the time passed without incident. Other than checking the perimeter of the building every so often, there was nothing to do but wait, nothing to focus on but the walls that seemed to close in with each passing hour.

And Maggie.

She sat on the other side of the kitchen table, the articles spread in front of her, taking notes in her precise handwriting he'd already seen whenever she'd given him a list of materials to pick up. He didn't know what she expected to find in the stories they'd already read numerous times or hoped to decipher from the day's events they'd already gone over a million times. Yet she continued, with the same unyielding persistence she'd shown with the house.

For the first time, he couldn't help appreciating her stubbornness. She certainly didn't give up when she put her mind to something. He had no doubt that if she'd been on the case to begin with, she wouldn't have rested until the killer had been caught. She'd be a good person to have on one's side, no matter the circumstances. Fierce. Tough. Loyal. He only wished she didn't sometimes waste that single-minded devotion on things that didn't deserve them, like this damned house.

As he watched, she paused in her writing to reread what she'd just committed to paper, lifting her head without looking up at him. A lock of blond hair had fallen over her cheek. She made no move to push it back, and for a ridiculous moment before he regained himself, his fingers twitched, itching to reach out and do it himself. Both the hair and her skin looked incredibly soft. He could only imagine what they'd feel like beneath his fingertips. Softer than anything he'd felt in a long time, no doubt. As soft as her mouth, now puckered slightly as she appeared to bite the inside of her lip in concentration...

He abruptly pushed away from the table. "I guess there's no harm in doing another check around the house this soon."

Maggie looked up in surprise, then nodded and began to climb to her feet. "All right."

"You don't have to get up," he said quickly. "I can do it."

She arched a brow. "You wouldn't let me go out there by myself, would you?"

"No."

She smiled sweetly. "So what makes you think I'd let you do the same?"

"I'll be fine."

"As would I. You'll be even better with somebody watching your back." Her eyes sparkled with amusement as she picked up her flashlight and moved toward the doorway. "Come on, tough guy. Let's go."

A reluctant smile nearly pulled at his mouth before he killed it. Though he didn't want to admit it, even to himself, he liked this woman. On a simple, basic level, he just flat-out liked her. And somehow that was more dangerous than the way he responded to how she looked. Or smelled, he acknowledged as she stepped past him, the faint trace of her scent reaching his nose and filling his senses.

With a sigh, he followed her down the hall in silence. It was the tedium that was getting to him, the lack of anything else to think about. He just needed to find something else to focus on.

They'd left the rest of the lights off to save energy. There was no point having them on. Everyone in town probably knew they were in here, and whoever had attacked Maggie had proved that knowledge wasn't scaring them off. Having all the lights on wasn't going to do any better.

So they moved in darkness, their steps echoing in the high ceiling and empty spaces, the sound of their soft, hushed breathing eerie in the stillness. A shudder worked through him as his eyes scanned the shadows of this place that was so familiar to him. His nightmares had been like this, walking through this house in the dark, not knowing who else might be out there, fearing who was. Not even Maggie's presence and the knowledge that he wasn't alone did anything to abate the familiar emotions. He swallowed, nearly feeling a cold sweat break out on his brow. He almost wished he could turn on a light, but didn't know how he'd explain the need to her.

In the front entryway, Maggie stopped to check that the front door remained locked. An unnecessary precaution perhaps, but an automatic one. Sam started to turn to the right to check the windows in the room there and make sure no one had managed to open one without their noticing.

Sam didn't know exactly what warned him. The instinct kicked in automatically, the sudden knowledge striking him with a certainty he felt in his bones.

Something was wrong.

He stopped abruptly, eyes narrowed as he tried to figure out what it was. Nothing appeared out of place. He listened closely, thinking it must have been a sound. He heard nothing. That left—

Even as he said it, Maggie froze, having just turned away from the door to face him. "Do you smell something?"

His first impulse was to say no. All he smelled was the scent of dust and wood that hung so heavily in the air in these front rooms. And her.

Then he realized that lurking beneath them was something else, something so faint it took him a few moments to recognize it was there at all. Then several more for his brain to make the connection and him to place it.

Gasoline.

He saw from the sudden widening of her eyes that she recognized it at the same time he did.

There was no time for either of them to say anything or react further. In the next instant, they heard a low roar, then a flash of light erupted outside the window, filling the room with a stark orange glow.

Neither of them had to say a word. They both knew what had happened.

Someone had set a fire.

They bolted for the door in unison, Maggie getting there first. He rushed out the door after her, almost slamming into her when she rounded the corner of the house and suddenly skidded to a halt. Maggie screamed.

Half the side wall was on fire, flames licking up from the ground to midway up the wall.

She started to lunge forward. He hooked an arm around her waist, holding her back. "We have to get out of here! It's too dangerous!"

"No! I won't leave it!"

She twisted in his arms, driving an elbow straight into his ribs. Holding back a groan, he struggled to maintain his hold on her. "We don't know how much gasoline they used. The whole place could go up any second!"

"I won't let it be destroyed! I can't! I won't let him do this! I won't!"

"Maggie—"

"Let me go!" she screamed, battering at his chest with her fists.

"Maggie, listen to me. I can get the hose, but I need to know you're not going to do anything stupid while I do."

It took a few seconds for the words to sink in, for her to meet his eyes. She nodded jerkily, first once, then several times, harder. "Please," she whispered hoarsely.

The word was so raw, so desperate, a chill slid through him. He didn't let the feeling sink in. He released her. When she didn't immediately dash toward the fire, simply staring at him with that look in her eyes, he turned and ran to the rear of the house.

He'd seen the hose coiled up back here before, but had no idea how long it was. He could only hope long enough. The valve didn't give easily, forcing him to apply extra effort to get it to loosen, then turn it as much as he could in a few twists of the wrist. Water immediately began to gush through the hose with gratifying pressure. If the hose wasn't long enough, maybe there was enough pressure that the water would reach anyway.

Grabbing the hose, he darted back around the side of the house and aimed the nozzle at the blaze. In the short time he'd been gone it seemed to have grown by a disturbing amount. A jolt shot through him as the water struck the building. He braced both legs shoulder-width apart to steady himself.

At first, the garden hose seemed a poor match for the fire, and the situation felt hopeless. But almost before he knew it, the flames began to die down, the water managing to conquer the fire. Maybe the arsonist hadn't had time to set the blaze properly, maybe Sam had simply lucked out and chosen the correct approach. However it happened, he managed to put out the fire, a shuddering breath working its way from his lungs when it realized it was actually happening.

Only when the flames were entirely extinguished did he have time to catch a breath and regain his thoughts. He suddenly realized that Maggie had done what he asked and stayed out of the way. In fact, he hadn't heard her say a word. He turned to look for her.

He spotted her standing a few yards behind him, staring at the wall that had been ablaze moments ago. It was too dark for her to see anything, but she continued staring, her gaze unmoving.

Her expression was more defeated than anything he'd ever seen from her. Even yesterday, when she'd declared that no one cared about what happened to her, she hadn't looked this crushed. He finally recognized that her cheeks were glistening, tears slowly sliding down her face. He remembered her frantic screams, the way she'd fought him in her desperation to save the house. The utter desolation on her face made it seem as if she hadn't even noticed that it had been saved. He couldn't imagine her looking more devastated if the whole house had burned to the ground, and God knew, he didn't want to. Even seeing it now sent a jolt through him that was more terrifying than anything he'd felt when the fire had seemed like it was out of control.

Dropping the hose, he slowly stepped toward her. She didn't react to his approach, simply standing there, eyes on the house.

"Maggie, the fire's out," he said carefully.

She didn't immediately respond. Finally, when he was about to reach out and touch her shoulder, she nodded slowly. "Thank you," she said, her voice still hoarse from all those screams.

He wanted to take her by the shoulders and shake her until she snapped out of it. *It's just a house,* he wanted to tell her. But more than ever before, it was clear from her reaction that it wasn't just a house, not to her.

Last night's intruder might have inflicted physical damage on her, but it was obvious whoever had set the fire had hurt her just as much, if not more.

And Sam vowed that before the night was through, he was going to find out once and for all what the bond was between Maggie and this damned house.

Chapter Ten

It was a half hour after the fire was out before anyone showed up in response to the blaze. Not the fire department. Not curious or concerned neighbors. Just a single police vehicle that slowly pulled up and parked in front of the house.

A lone officer stepped from behind the driver's seat and walked toward Sam and Maggie. Sam recognized him even before his face became visible.

Clearly Maggie did, too. The man was still a dozen yards away when she called out, "Evening, Chief. Though, I guess that should be 'Good morning' by now."

Sam jerked his head. "Chief?" He scanned Nate from head to toe, paying closer attention to his uniform, something he evidently should have done during their earlier encounters. It hadn't even occurred to him.

"John, this is Police Chief Nate Cassidy," Maggie said when Nate came close enough. "Chief, John Samuels."

Nate grimaced, the lights they'd turned on in the

house illuminating a dangerous glint in his stare as his eyes met Sam's. He nodded, not offering his hand. "Samuels." Without waiting for a response, he turned toward the fire damage. "Did the fire department already take off? They might all be volunteers, but it looks like they got the job done before it could spread too quickly."

"*John* got the job done," Maggie said. "The fire department never showed up."

Nate's brow furrowed. "Never showed up? That's hard to believe. The volunteer fire department was first formed almost thirty years ago after someone died in a house fire. Since then, no one in Fremont has died in a fire and no home has ever been lost. They take great pride in that. I've never heard of them not showing up at a fire before. Maybe you put it out so quickly they didn't hear about it."

"*You* heard about it," Maggie pointed out. "More likely they just decided having this house burn wouldn't be any great loss. That seems to be the popular opinion in town."

"I'm afraid I can't argue with you there." He glanced between them. "I hear the two of you have been running around asking some uncomfortable questions."

"Who told you that?" Sam asked.

"Several people."

"People who sounded upset enough to set fire to the house because of those questions?" Sam demanded.

"You think that's why this happened tonight?"

"I don't think it's a coincidence that the very day we start asking questions, somebody tries burning the house down. Especially a day after someone broke in and attacked Maggie."

Nate shot a glance at Maggie. "I didn't hear about that."

"I didn't report it," she said, stone-faced. "I didn't think there was much of a point."

"It would be better to have it on the record in case this person is caught."

"And what are the chances of that, Chief? The police department doesn't have the best history when it comes to catching people, does it?"

"I can see why you would think that, but we take assaults on people very seriously."

"Just not vandalism like the other incidents at the house?"

"Just because there's nothing I can do doesn't mean I'm happy about it. We're a small department with limited resources. There's no real evidence indicating who's responsible for the damage. I also can't afford to have anyone staking out your house, any more than you said you could afford the surveillance cameras I suggested if you're really interested in catching whoever's responsible."

Maggie frowned, but she didn't disagree. "At least this time you have a place to start. Chances are, one of the people who were upset by our questions did this. Several of them were certainly angry enough to do it."

"We don't know that," Nate said. "For all we know

this is just the result of kids pulling a prank, the way they have on this house for years. This one could have just gotten out of hand."

"You don't really believe that," Sam said before Maggie could voice the outrage that was written all over her face.

"Not really, no," Nate admitted. "But someone has to be clear-headed around here instead of running around half-cocked, throwing around a bunch of theories with no proof."

"At least someone *is* asking questions," Maggie said. "Someone should have been asking them for the past thirty years."

Nate sighed. "Ms. Harper, believe me, I'm as interested in solving that case as anyone who ever worked for the Fremont PD, if not more. I looked at the file myself as soon as I joined the department. But there's only so much we can do without any new information or leads. Sometimes a case just goes cold and asking the same questions isn't going to do any good. Frankly, I'd wager that nothing you've asked hasn't been asked before. I heard you had a run-in with Paul Winslow, most likely about the fact that you talked to his daughter. I assume it was about the argument he had with Greg and Emily Ross the weekend before the murders, and most likely the fact that Teri Winslow had a key to the house. I also know Clay Howell was in an uproar because Samuels here went to talk to Janet, which means you probably know about the whole grudge between him and Greg Ross. Did I miss anything?"

The way Maggie's mouth hardened into a thin line, she didn't like having to admit it any more than he did. "No," she finally said.

"Well, there you go," Nate said. "Look, if you find out anything new, I would be happy to hear it. But I firmly believe everyone who worked this case did so to the best of their abilities. There's just never been any way to prove who killed the Rosses."

Sam wanted to rail against Nate's words, knowing exactly the same frustration Maggie was clearly feeling. It wasn't easy to accept the idea that everyone had done exactly what they were supposed to and everything they could, and yet the case had still never been solved. It just wasn't supposed to be that way. But then, what exactly in life did go the way it was supposed to?

"So what are you going to do about the fire?" Maggie asked.

"Everything I can," he said firmly. "I'll get some of my guys out here, we'll collect as much evidence as we can, and we'll talk to the neighbors. Are you going to be around?"

"Yes," Maggie said, at the same time Sam said, "No."

Her eyes flew to his. "I'm not going anywhere."

"You need to get some rest," he said just as vehemently. "Not to mention we both reek of smoke. I never did check out of the motel, so I've got my room there. We can shower, get some rest. Whoever did this isn't going to come back tonight."

"You don't know that, any more than you knew

that they were going to set the fire in the first place. Neither of us did."

"I'll stick around until morning if it'll make you feel better," Nate said, surprising them both. "I doubt I'm going to be getting any sleep the rest of the night as it is." He exhaled slowly, the breath heavy with frustration. "I hate that this is happening here. You might not believe me, but this is usually a nice town. Your grandparents must have thought so, too, having lived here so long. Things like this don't happen here."

From the look on her face, he was right. She didn't believe him. Maggie stared at him, as though trying to decide whether to trust him. Sam could tell she didn't want to. But not even she could deny the sincerity in Nate's words.

"Thank you," she said finally, the comment heartfelt enough that Sam felt a ridiculous spurt of jealousy. The thanks she'd given him for saving the house hadn't contained nearly as much emotion. "That would make me feel better."

"Glad to help, then," Nate said with a nod.

"Come on," Sam said. "Let's get out of here and let the man do his job." On the last words, he pinned Nate with a look, hopefully leaving no doubt he wanted the man to do just that.

Nate stared back like he didn't even know him. He glanced from Sam to Maggie and back again, then turned away and headed back to his car with a barely perceptible shake of his head.

Whether or not Nate had read his signal, Sam

understood that one loud and clear. Sam had no room giving orders or passing judgments here. He was the one outright lying to Maggie. She would likely be far angrier with him than she was with Nate if she learned how he'd deceived her.

Even as he thought it, she glanced up at him, her face so weary, so vulnerable, his heart clutched in his chest. "Okay," she agreed. "Let's go."

There was nothing he could do but push down the regret simmering more forcefully than ever in his gut and get her out of there.

JOHN's room was at the same motel Maggie had checked into when she first arrived in the area, one outside of Fremont proper and closer to the highway. She'd chosen it because she'd wanted to be able to escape the prying eyes of the townspeople as much as possible when she went home at night. That was really all there was to recommend about the place. Seeing it now, it was as unimpressive as Maggie remembered. The rooms were small and slightly dingy with outdated furniture in questionable shape, but at that moment, no place could have looked more like paradise.

Her initial relief gave way to trepidation as soon as she saw the single queen-size bed in the center of the room. She glanced back at John, standing in the doorway behind her. "I don't mind taking the floor," she said. "I've been sleeping on one long enough back at the house."

"Take the bed," he said roughly. "I'll take the chair."

She finally noticed the chair sitting next to a table beside the window. It didn't exactly look suitable for a good night's sleep. "Are you sure? You deserve the bed after everything you did tonight."

"The chair's fine," he said, his tone allowing no further argument.

She didn't have the energy to give him one. She gratefully sank onto the edge of the bed and listened to him lock the door. It was all she could do not to fall back against the bedspread and close her eyes. She had no doubt she would be asleep within moments if she did.

"What was that tonight?"

Maggie glanced up in surprise to find John still standing, leaning back against the door. He was staring at her, his arms folded across his chest.

She knew what he was talking about, of course. She tried not to fidget under the force of his unwavering gaze. She still turned away from it, lowering her head. She felt it just the same.

"Somebody set fire to the house," she said as calmly as she could. "Weren't you paying attention?"

"Yes, I was. I was paying attention when you almost got yourself killed in that fire."

"We were nowhere close to being in that much danger," she scoffed.

"Are you a fire expert? Because I've seen a bad fire before and there's no predicting how one is going to unfold. The whole building could have gone up before either of us realized it and had any chance of getting away. And all you could think about was blindly running toward that fire with no plan of what you were going to do."

"What was I supposed to do? Just stand by and do nothing while the coward who set the fire got exactly what they wanted?"

"It's just a house. It's not worth your life."

"It's not just a house."

"Then what is it? Because I damn well don't see what's worth risking your life for in that place."

She wanted to offer another denial. That stubborn streak that had gotten her in trouble more times than she could count demanded she do just that.

But as she opened her mouth to do it, she suddenly couldn't. The only sound that emerged from between her lips was a sigh.

She was too tired. The weariness hit her all at once, until she felt nothing else. After the night she'd had, after the weeks of dealing with the townspeople, after the year of pretending she was fine when she really wasn't, she suddenly just couldn't pretend anymore. Even one more lie would require more energy than she could begin to muster.

"You're right," she said softly. "It's not really about the house. I may be pathetic, but I have some self-awareness."

"Then what is it about?"

The harshness had faded from his tone, leaving a gentleness that surprised her. That unexpected tenderness practically coaxed the confession from her throat, words she never thought would be so easy, so simple to say.

"It's about my marriage." Even as she said it, she felt the humiliation burn her face.

"What happened with your marriage?" John asked, somehow even more gently than before.

She took a steadying breath. "My husband left me. He came home one day and said it was over. He was in love with somebody else. And that was that."

Strange how the words seem to flow off her tongue as though they were meaningless. She expected to feel that same searing pain that used to rip through her whenever she thought about that day, the agony that had only just started to subside. Instead, that overwhelming weariness provided a comforting numbness, insulating her from the confession's true impact.

"You didn't see it coming?"

"Not a clue. I thought we were happy. Things weren't perfect—I mean, what is?—but they were good. At least I thought so. And then one day he just walked away and never looked back."

Maggie shook her head, the memories of that day returning to her mind with painful vividness. "We didn't even fight. I know how out of character that must seem for me. I was just so blindsided by the whole thing. I was in the kitchen, making dinner, and everything was normal. Then he came home, said he was leaving, and that was that. He went upstairs and packed a bag and left, and I just stood there. I didn't fight for him. I didn't fight for the marriage.

I just stood there and did nothing. Because I didn't understand what was happening. Because it didn't make any sense."

She sucked in a breath, her lungs so painfully tight it hurt to do so. "I probably shouldn't have been as shocked as I was. I mean, people get divorced all the time. You always hear about the divorce rate in this country. But my parents stayed together. So did my grandparents. Maybe if they hadn't I would have been prepared for the idea that my marriage might not last forever. But I wasn't. It never occurred to me that it could happen to me. So I just stood there and watched him walk out the door.

"It's just not supposed to be that way. I know we live in a disposable society these days, but some things are supposed to last, you know? It doesn't matter if it's marriage, or houses, or whatever. When you build something, it's supposed to last. You don't just throw it away because it's not perfect anymore, or because something better has—or could—come along. Some things are supposed to *last*."

To her mortification she felt her eyes begin to burn. A tear slipped free before she could do anything about it, stinging as it made its way down her cheek. She made no move to wipe it away, unable to find the strength to do so much as raise her hand. The sense of helplessness that weighed down on her, threatening to crush her as it had for so long, was too much to shake.

"I hate this. I hate that it still hurts a year later. I hate that I can't stop thinking about it, and the only

time I do is when I'm thinking about the house.
I hate that he's moved on so easily, like nothing's
changed at all. I hate that he's happy and I'm...*lost*.
I hate that he threw away something that was supposed to be forever."

She finally raised her head and looked at him.
"Tell me, how does somebody do that? How do you
just walk away like it's nothing, like it never mattered
at all?"

This time it was he who lowered his eyes, shifting
uncomfortably from one foot to the other. "I'm sorry.
I couldn't tell you."

That's right, she realized. He was exactly the
wrong person to ask. He was a drifter, a man who
appeared to be forty years old and had no apparent ties. He didn't expect anything to be permanent.
Even now he was just passing through. He would be
leaving soon, too.

"Maybe you're better off that way," she said.

He chuckled humorlessly. "I don't know about
that," he said, his voice was thick with emotion.

"At least that way you can't get hurt."

He grimaced as though he wanted to disagree with
her. She waited for him to do so, wanted to know
what he was about to say. But when he finally spoke,
all he said was, "Maybe your husband was just a
jerk."

"I don't think so. And if he is, that doesn't say
much for my judgment. I'd known him since we
were eleven years old. We'd been together since we
were fifteen. I never wanted to be with anyone else,

never thought I would be." She shrugged. "Maybe I won't. If you can't really know who someone is after twenty years, what's the chance you'll ever really know them?"

"People change."

"True. And not always for the better. I'm not sure that's much comfort."

"Did you ever ask him? Why he cheated? Why he left?"

"No. How pathetic would that be? Not to mention I was afraid of the answer." She sighed. "Look, I know I'm not nice and sweet. I have a big mouth and I say what I think, even when I probably shouldn't." She winced. "He always said he liked that about me."

"You don't believe him?"

"It's hard to when he went out and replaced me with somebody who *is* all nice and sweet."

He snorted, making her look up in surprise. "She can't be too nice and sweet. Nice, sweet women don't get involved with other women's husbands."

"So she fakes it better than I do." It was her turn to snort. "I have a feeling it's not the only thing that's fake about her, starting with her hair color and ending with those ridiculous things bouncing around in her bra—at least when she wears one." She shot him an apologetic look. "See? That wasn't nice."

To her surprise, one corner of his mouth slowly curved upward in the faint beginnings of a smile. "Maybe not, but I think you're entitled to say it."

It certainly wasn't much of one, but the sight of that near half smile actually made her feel a completely unexpected twinge in her chest. He'd been so solemn the entire time she'd known him. In fact, she couldn't recall a single instance when he'd cracked a grin. It was a shame. Even that slight smile lightened his face, hinting at the promise of what a true smile would be like. Her heart lurched in her chest, then started to beat faster. She suspected it would be breathtaking. And suddenly, more than anything, she wished she could see it.

"Thank you for that," she said. "And for everything else. You've really gone above and beyond. By now, I probably owe you hazard pay for everything you've done."

"I didn't do any of it because you're paying me."

"Why did you do it?"

He lapsed into silence, lowering his eyes. "It seemed like the right thing to do."

She let the words sink in, slowly considering their meaning. Finally she shook her head, laughing softly.

He raised his eyes. "You don't believe me?"

"Actually I do," she said. "I just realized that the idea of somebody doing the right thing seems so strange to me, and it struck me how sad that is."

He simply surveyed her silently for a long moment.

"You should get some sleep," he said roughly. "You look like you're about to pass out."

She laughed drily. "Not too surprising, since I feel like it."

"Get some sleep," he said again. "It'll be morning soon enough."

He was right. Just thinking of everything that faced her in the morning sent a fresh wave of exhaustion washing over her. She crawled up on the bed and curled up on the mattress. In the back of her mind, she vaguely registered that she should shower. He'd been right earlier. They both smelled of smoke. But she couldn't bring herself to even do that.

The only thing that seemed to matter was closing her eyes and finally forgetting everything for as long as she could.

It didn't take long for Maggie to drift to sleep. It wasn't exactly a deep sleep. Even as Sam watched, she shifted restlessly on the bed, uneasy even in slumber. Regardless of the quality, she could use all the rest she could get.

Sleep was nowhere close to coming for him. He sat in the chair next to the window, his back to it. He could have turned on the TV, but didn't want to disturb her. So he just sat there, wide-awake.

And watched her.

As soon as he realized he was doing it, he forced himself to look away, to look at anything else, even if there really wasn't much else to look at in the simple motel room.

And for what seemed like the hundredth time, he found his gaze drawn back to her before he realized it.

Finally, he forced himself to stop fighting the inevitable and let his gaze linger.

She was on her side, facing him, her face clearly visible. Her hair wasn't tied up anymore, and a few locks fell over her cheek. She really was pretty. And smart. And tough. And several other things he couldn't help like about her no matter how much he wanted to. He wondered what kind of idiot could leave a woman like this.

It was a strange thought. He'd never met a woman he couldn't leave. Never met anyone he couldn't say goodbye to, if he bothered saying it at all.

But then, he'd made sure nobody got hurt when he left by being damn careful about the kind of women he got involved with in the first place. Women with their bright eyes and open expressions and friendly smiles—he stayed the hell away from those women. They were the ones who still believed in goodness and kindness and happy endings. Those women hadn't been hurt yet, not really, and he sure as hell wasn't going to be the one to do it. He'd hurt enough people, even before his twelfth birthday.

The only women he had any business getting involved with, even for a short time, were those who'd seen the world and the people in it for what they were, who didn't expect anything because they knew better than to from anybody, the way he did. When it was time for him to move on, there were no tears or anger or hurt feelings, only the knowledge that they'd arrived at an ending they'd both known was inevitable from the very beginning.

This woman was different. She didn't fit so easily into a simple category. Maybe it was because she'd been hurt so recently that it hadn't sunk in yet. Maybe because she was a fighter, enough that it wasn't going to beat her, not entirely. Even if she didn't know it yet, she hadn't given up. She'd been bruised by the experience, but not beaten. Her wounds would heal without leaving scars, and she would come out stronger and wiser. That was, if she wasn't hurt again, an injury inflicted on a still-festering one that went deeper still and wouldn't heal. That's what would happen if she was burned again by another man who lied to her, the way he already was.

Another man who walked away. And in the end, that was all he could do.

He knew it. It was more than enough reason for him to look away. That was what he should do, for her sake. He knew that, too.

But he didn't do it. Despite the instinct telling him to do exactly that, another one—fiercer, harder to resist, and for reasons he couldn't hope to explain—kept his steady gaze right on her.

Where it remained until morning.

Chapter Eleven

Maggie had expected the fire damage to look even worse in the light of day than it had the night before. To her surprise—and substantial relief—it didn't. Rather than mask the destruction, the darkness had merely kept her from seeing that it wasn't so bad after all. Most of the damage had been limited to a relatively small section of the house, and there didn't appear to be any major structural damage. Maggie knew she had John to thank for that, and for so many other things, no matter how much she didn't want that to be the case.

The man himself had gone to pick up some supplies from the hardware store, leaving her alone with the house—and her embarrassment for pouring her heart out the night before. She hadn't discussed the end of her marriage so openly with anyone, and she had to admit it had been something of a relief to finally do so. But she still barely knew the man, and though he hadn't said anything, she knew it must have been embarrassing for him, as well, to hear the intimate details of her life. She'd barely been able to face him that morning, and had been a little glad when he'd left so she could get some breathing room and forget how she'd behaved the night before.

And now she was alone, with something more important to focus on.

The house.

She stepped back and continued to survey the damage, mentally calculating the repairs that would need to be made and any supplies that would be required beyond the list she'd sent John off with. It wouldn't be easy, but it could be far worse, and the repairs would get done. She almost reached out and patted the wall reassuringly, as if to comfort the house, as well, as herself. A foolish impulse, no doubt, but she was beyond denying the strange kinship she felt with this place. She and the house had both taken their hits from people determined to knock them down, but they were still standing. And they were going to stay that way, she thought fiercely. No matter what it took.

The sound of a vehicle slowing to a stop drew her attention away from the house. It was too soon for John to have returned. As soon as she recognized the car, she nearly threw her head back and groaned.

Dalton. She should have known.

Swallowing her irritation, she watched him climb out of his car, his smile bigger than ever, an extra spring in his step as he started toward her. Seeing his good mood and knowing its cause, it was all she could do not to snarl as he approached.

Instead, she sucked in a breath, forcing herself to

stay calm. Managing a smile that no doubt looked as fake as it felt, she spoke first, determined to knock some of that cockiness out of his swagger. "Good morning, Dalton. I've been expecting you."

To her supreme satisfaction, his smile slipped slightly and he missed a step. "Oh, really?"

"Of course. In the wake of something bad happening, it's only natural for the vultures to descend."

If he was offended at being called a vulture, he hid it well, his smile sliding back into place. "Well, I admit I did hear about last night's unfortunate events—"

"Uh-huh. You wouldn't happen to know anything about who's responsible for those unfortunate events, would you?"

He did an admirable job feigning indignation. "Of course not. I have to tell you I'm offended you would even suggest such a thing."

"Then it's a shame I couldn't care less about offending you."

"Me or anyone else, it would seem. Because it sure looks like you've offended somebody."

"For having the audacity to try renovating my own house?"

"Or for running around town, asking questions people don't like."

"Does that include you, Dalton? Because there's really only one person who shouldn't like the questions I'm asking."

"Nobody likes being accused of a crime, especially if they're innocent."

"And especially if they're guilty, I would imagine."

"It sounds like you're imagining a lot of things, you and that man working for you, the way you're throwing around accusations."

"I haven't been accusing anyone. I've just been asking questions. And here's one I've been wanting to ask you. I hear that Greg Ross worked for you. Funny how you never mentioned that."

His smile tightened. "No reason I should," he said stiffly. "It was a long time ago."

"So were the murders, and people around here can't seem to stop mentioning them. Tell me about Greg Ross. Why would someone want to kill him and his wife?"

"I'm not interested in helping you play detective."

"I'm not interested in selling you my house. That hasn't stopped you from asking."

"And you haven't entertained any of my generous offers for the house. So there's no reason I should indulge your questions."

"We both know why I haven't entertained your offers. What I don't know is why you wouldn't be willing to answer a simple question."

"Because those poor folks deserve to rest in peace," he snapped. "They don't deserve to have their tragedy dragged out and rehashed because you're too stubborn for your own good."

"Really? It's not because you may have had a motive to kill them?"

The man's jaw dropped, the shock too thorough

to be fake. "Me? What the hell are you talking about?"

"I hear you got into trouble a few years after Greg and Emily Ross were murdered. Something about the discovery that a house built by your company contained substandard materials?"

"That had nothing to do with me. I made the mistake of taking on a partner who I shouldn't have trusted. I was personally cleared of any involvement."

"On that project. But it was built about the same time this house was, wasn't it? Did Greg Ross find something wrong with this house?"

"Of course not!"

"Really? Because I've never seen someone so eager to destroy something they built themselves. Is that why you're so opposed to me renovating it? Is it because you're afraid I'll find something wrong with it structurally? Is that why you want to tear it down?"

"I want to tear it down because I hate the damn place!"

"Why would you hate something you built yourself?"

"It's because I built it, you fool. It's because I'm the reason they were living here, in this damned house where they were killed!"

Whatever she'd expected him to say, that certainly wasn't it. "What are you talking about?"

"I'm the one who hooked them up with your grand-dad. Yeah, I built it for him. I knew he hated seeing the house empty and didn't want to sell. I knew Greg and Emily were looking for a place. They were still young, they had all those kids and couldn't afford a big enough place for all of them. So I came up with the bright idea that they should rent from your grand-dad. The best solution for everybody. Do you think I would have had them bring a bunch of kids to live here if I'd thought there was something wrong with the house?" He sucked in a ragged breath. "And then it turned out the way it did."

Seeing Dalton's face, stripped of its usual bravado, utterly shattered, shook her more than his words. Sympathy, something she never thought she would ever feel for Dalton Sterling, twisted in her gut.

"I'm sorry. I didn't know."

He snorted softly. "Yeah, well, there's a lot you don't know. You didn't know these people, but they were good people who didn't deserve what happened to them. But you don't care about that. All you care about is this house."

"I do care. I don't think they deserve to be forgotten and ignored."

"No, they don't. But they also don't deserve to be remembered only for the way they died. And that's what this house is, a living reminder that those two people were brutally killed. As long as this house is here, it's all people will remember."

She almost expected that to be another prelude for him to make an offer on the house. Instead, he simply turned and started toward his car.

Halfway there, he suddenly stopped and looked

back, his expression grave. "I've been checking into that man you hired."

"I had a feeling you would. You weren't exactly subtle when you stopped to take down his license plate number the other day."

"What exactly do you know about him?"

"He's a good worker, and he has no interest in running me out of town. That's all I need to know."

"So you didn't know his truck is registered to a man named Mike Bryant?"

No, she hadn't, she thought, unable to suppress a tiny twinge of dread. She recognized the name. Mike Bryant was the reference John had provided her. She'd spoken to the man herself. But why was John driving the man's truck?

She never let her bravado waver. "You know, I never thought to ask."

"That doesn't bother you? The fact that he's driving somebody else's truck?"

"Was the truck reported stolen?"

Dalton frowned, his unhappiness at the answer immediately boosting her mood before she heard it. "No."

"Then there's no reason it should."

"Look, I know we got off on the wrong foot, but I truly mean you no harm, Maggie. And before you dismiss what I'm saying out of hand, I'm going to ask you to think about what I have to say. There's something off about that guy. I can't put my finger on it, but something about him doesn't add up. Just think about it before you go trusting him."

With that, he continued back to his car. Maggie watched in silence as he pulled out of the driveway and headed off down the street.

She wanted to do exactly as he'd predicted and dismiss what he'd said without another thought. But as much as she'd like to, she couldn't.

She'd meant what she'd said to Dalton. The fact that John was driving someone else's truck, someone to whom he was close and who thought enough of him to serve as a reference, shouldn't bother her in the least.

Which didn't explain why it did.

She couldn't explain it, even to herself. She hated the fact that she was doubting him, hated that she was letting something that Dalton Sterling, of all people, had said bother her. But like something caught between her teeth that she couldn't seem to loosen, the question nagged at her long after Dalton left.

Why was John driving another man's truck? There were two people she could ask, and she wasn't sure she could wait until John's return. She still had Mike Bryant's phone number.

Before she could even think about it, she pulled out the number and reached for the phone.

She held her breath as the line rang, hoping she didn't get his answering machine or voice mail. As with the first time they'd spoken, the man himself answered around the fourth ring.

"Mr. Bryant, this is Maggie Harper. We spoke a

few days ago about a man named John Samuels, who I was considering hiring to work on my house."

"Of course, Ms. Harper," he said. "Is everything all right?"

He sounded exactly the same as the first time they'd spoken, except this time she recognized something she remembered but hadn't registered then, a certain guarded note in his seemingly friendly tone.

"Yes, it is. John's worked out just fine so far," she said, deciding to skip how much his responsibilities had expanded or how above and beyond he'd gone in the past few days. Just thinking about it made her feel a pang of guilt for checking up on him. She pushed the feeling aside and made herself plow on. "I was just wondering about something."

"What's that, Ms. Harper?" This time there was no missing that guarded note or the tinge of wariness.

"I have to admit, a friend of mine did a little checking up on John—" she couldn't help but roll her eyes at the lie "—and he found out that the truck John's driving is actually registered in your name."

"That's true," he said without hesitation. "I lent John my truck."

His confirmation made her feel foolish for calling. He made it sound like such a simple thing, which it really was.

Stumped, she struggled for something to say, some way to address her concerns. "When you vouched for him, I didn't realize how close you must be for you to be willing to lend him your truck for an extended amount of time."

"If you're worried about him taking off and cutting out on the job early on you, don't be. John will stick around until the job is done."

He was telling her what he thought she wanted to hear. Was that what he'd done before?

"So he didn't tell you when to expect it back?"

"He didn't need to. I trust him. Heck, I would trust Sam with my life. We actually served together—the Army. It's not something he'd ever admit to, but he did save my life. Lending him the truck is the least I could do for all I owe him."

She barely heard most of his comments. "Sam," she repeated with a frown. "You call him Sam?"

There was a noticeable silence on the other end of the line before Mike Bryant chuckled, the noise sounding distinctly forced. "A nickname. Just something his friends call him. I hope you won't be offended if he didn't ask you to call him by it."

"You called him John the first time we spoke."

"Because you did. And because it's his name."

Again, there was a distinct—and, she thought, telling—pause between the first sentence and the last, as though the latter had been added as an afterthought.

"Thank you, Mr. Bryant. You've been very helpful."

He started to say something else, perhaps recognizing the edge in her voice and trying to sound reassuring. She didn't bother to listen, cutting off the call.

She stood there, mulling it over in her mind as the sense of unease that had been building at the base of her skull intensified. It wasn't the fact that the man called John by another name, one that made perfect sense for the name she knew. Men always seemed to be giving each other nicknames, calling each other shortened versions of their last names. It was a guy thing. She'd been around enough men to know that. John was a fairly common name, so naturally a friend would call him something more personal, and if Sam wasn't the most creative spin on the last name Samuels, it made enough sense to work. And because he'd introduced himself as a prospective employee, not a friend, naturally he would give her his full name rather than a nickname.

No, the use of a different name didn't bother her.

It was the fact that the name was familiar.

Sam…

Another fairly common name, but also one she was sure she'd come across somewhere recently. But where…

Like a puzzle piece falling into place, she remembered where she'd seen that name.

Her heart plummeted into her stomach. As soon as it came to her, the significance of what it meant hit her like a blow to the gut.

Desperately wanting to believe she was wrong, hoping that she hadn't let herself be made a fool by another man, she quickly moved to the table and the newspaper articles still spread out on top of it. She sifted through the papers, trying to remember which one she was looking for. She had almost pushed it aside when she found it. She froze, one hand braced on top of the paper, her thumb and forefinger bracketing the words.

And there it was, so blatantly obvious Maggie felt like every inch the idiot she clearly was.

Greg and Emily Ross had five sons. Gideon was the oldest, the one who wasn't home that night. That left four who were. Luke, Jacob, Joshua.

And Sam.

SAM was loading the last of his bags from the hardware store into the back of the pickup truck when he spotted Janet Howell heading toward him on the sidewalk. Her head bent, she hadn't noticed him yet.

He called out. "Mrs. Howell."

She jerked her head up, clearly startled, glancing in every direction for the person who'd said her name. When she saw him, her pale face seemed to go even whiter, her eyes widening. Appearing very much like a deer in the headlights, she looked as if she wanted nothing more than to turn and run from him.

He quickly dropped the bag in the truck and started toward her before she could move. "Can I have a word with you?"

"I don't think we have anything to talk about."

"Your ex-husband came to see my boss and me yesterday. He said you informed him I came to see you."

"That's right. I thought he should know."

"I had the impression the two of you weren't very close."

"We're not. But he was my husband. It seemed the decent thing to inform him somebody was running around, wanting to accuse him of murder."

"He wasn't too happy."

"Did you think he would be?"

"Actually, he seemed more upset that we talked to you than that I wanted to talk to him. Does that make sense to you?"

She swallowed. "I—I don't know."

"Can you think of a reason why he wouldn't want me talking to you?"

There was a noticeable pause before she uttered a hoarse, completely unconvincing, "No."

He decided to take a different tack. "Mrs. Howell, you probably heard by now that somebody set fire to the house I'm working on last night."

She gave her head a wobbly shake. "No," she practically whispered. "I hadn't heard."

"Funny coincidence that it happened the same day your ex-husband told us we'd be sorry for talking to you. He seems like a very angry man. Do you think that's something he would do?"

"No," she said automatically, but with no more conviction. "He wouldn't. He—"

Suddenly, her eyes went past him, panic flashing across her face. Before he could glance behind himself to see what she was looking at, she started to back away.

"I can't talk to you. Please leave me alone."

She turned on her heel and hurried away down the sidewalk. Short of chasing her down and forcing her to speak with him, there didn't seem to be anything Sam could do.

He quickly glanced back over his shoulder, already fairly certain what he'd find. Clay Howell stood at the end of the sidewalk, far enough away that he wouldn't have been able to hear what they were talking about, close enough that he'd clearly seen them, judging from the rage on his face and in every inch of his tense posture. He didn't look the slightest bit nervous or guilty, simply furious in a way that sent a ripple of unease through Sam's system.

Bracing himself for the imminent confrontation, Sam wondered if he should wait for the man to come to him, or beat him to the punch and go to him. Nothing like keeping the enemy off-kilter.

He didn't get a chance to make up his mind. Howell suddenly spun around and stalked off in the other direction.

Surprise froze Sam in place. Before he could take a step forward, the man had turned a corner and disappeared from view.

Sam was tempted to go after him, but he doubted he'd catch him on foot. The man knew the town better than he did. Sam could probably track him down, but as much as he'd like to, he'd already spent enough time in town. Maggie would be wondering where he was.

Walking back to his truck, he climbed in and headed back to the house, Janet Howell's panic-stricken face lingering in his mind the whole way there.

THERE was no sign of Maggie when Sam pulled up in front of the house. He thought she might come out to help him unload the truck when she heard him, but she didn't appear. Wondering where she was, he picked up as many bags as he could and headed into the house.

That same feeling of dread he'd experienced the first day came over him, building with every step, the way it did every time he entered the house. He did his best to shake off the sensation, even if he couldn't do it completely. He wondered how long it would be before he got over the feeling. If three days wasn't enough to do it, he wondered if he ever would.

It didn't help that that same unsettling silence lay over the building. As he pushed open the door, he listened for any sounds of movement, any indication that Maggie was nearby.

He heard nothing. Only the eerie, endless squeal of the door's hinges as it slowly opened, the noise echoing through the empty rooms just beyond. He winced, the sound making his skin crawl. He should have oiled the hinges long ago.

"Maggie?" he called.

His voice resounded back at him. There was no response.

She obviously wasn't in any of the front rooms he could see from where he was standing. He heard none of the telltale squeaks from the ceiling he knew he would hear if someone was moving around up there. She probably wasn't upstairs.

His unease growing, he forced himself to head back toward the kitchen, the room he still had a hard time setting foot inside. Had something happened? Had her attacker come back? Had he made a mistake in leaving her alone?

He stepped carefully, wondering if someone was inside, listening to him approach. He debated dropping the bags. Maybe he should leave his arms free. He might need them if he was heading into an ambush.

He reached the kitchen before he'd made up his mind, and then the decision was made for him. He spotted her the instant he stepped into the room. He drew up in surprise just inside the doorway. Maggie was fine. She was sitting at the table, her head bowed, staring at the newspaper printouts spread across the surface.

He opened his mouth to ask why she hadn't answered him. Before he had the chance, she lifted her head, her eyes immediately finding his.

And he knew she wasn't fine at all.

The chill returned with a vengeance, and this time it had nothing to do with the house.

"Hello, *John,*" she said, and the little slant she threw on his name told him all he needed to know before she said another word.

She cocked her head. "Or do you prefer Sam? Because that is your real name. Isn't it, Samuel John Ross?"

Chapter Twelve

Maggie had had more than an hour to think about how she wanted this to unfold. She'd imagined catching him off-guard, throwing the truth of his identity, the secret he'd so carefully concealed, right in his face and laying into him until she made him feel as stupid as he had her. He wouldn't see it coming, would have no idea what was about to happen, and she would have the pleasure of seeing his embarrassment when he realized he hadn't pulled one over on her.

He didn't even give her the courtesy of embarrassment or shame. He simply stood there, two big paper bags in his arms, no expression whatsoever on his face, looking at her with those disarmingly blue eyes.

The lack of a reaction only made her angrier. She knew she'd caught him off-guard, but he was too contained to give her the satisfaction of embarrassment. But then, she'd probably overestimated the damage she could inflict. No matter what she said, the mere surprise of revealing she knew the truth he'd tried to hide couldn't hurt him as badly as he had her.

"Did you really think I was so stupid I wouldn't figure it out?"

"I didn't think about it at all, really," he said. He slowly bent over and set the bags on the floor. "None of this—coming back here, investigating what happened—was something I thought about. I just did it on the spur of the moment. I got in the truck and drove here. I saw your ad at the truck stop, I came here to see the house and I applied for the job. I didn't think about any of it. It just happened."

If she'd had anything on hand she would have thrown it at him. Lying to her all this time hadn't just *happened*. Letting her think he was helping her investigate what had happened here when he likely knew so much more about it than he ever said hadn't just *happened*. Listening to her reveal her deepest secrets about everything that had happened with Kevin while he was playing her just as much for a fool hadn't just *happened*.

She didn't let herself say any of it, not about to give him the satisfaction of turning into some over-emotional woman.

"Why?" she said simply, unable to completely keep the dangerous note out of that single word. "Why come back now after all this time?"

He didn't say anything for a long moment. Finally, he reached into his back pocket and pulled out something. Crossing the room, moving slowly as though he wasn't sure it was safe to approach—smart man—he handed it to her.

With some reluctance, she took it, careful to avoid contact with his fingers. The envelope was small and battered, worn around the edges from being handled quite a bit. It had probably been white when it had been sent, although those days were long past. It was addressed to Sam Ross in care of Mike Bryant—him again. She noted the postmark. It had been sent almost three months ago. The postmark said New York, but she didn't recognize the name of the town where it had been mailed.

She opened the flap and pulled out the card inside. It was a wedding invitation, she recognized immediately. Nothing fancy, just a simple card with plain type. It didn't list the name of the bride's and groom's parents like most wedding invitations. It was the bride and groom inviting the recipient to their wedding, with the date, time and location noted.

The name of the groom was equally recognizable. "Gideon," she recited. "Your brother's getting married."

She looked up when he didn't say anything. He nodded, his expression tight. "Yes."

"I don't understand," she said, barely managing to hold back her impatience. He was making her feel stupid again, not that the feeling had ever really faded. "What does this have to do with you being here?"

"I came as soon as I got it."

"What do you mean, as soon as you got this? It was sent months ago. The wedding's on Saturday."

"It took a while to get to me."

"Your friend Mike didn't give it to you?"

"Yeah, he did. Five days ago. He gave it to me. I asked if I could borrow his truck, and I came here."

He said it like it made sense. Maybe it did to him, a fact she didn't find all that reassuring. "Why didn't Mike give it to you sooner?"

"He didn't know where to find me. It's been a while since I've had a permanent address. I see Bryant every now and then. He gets mail for me, that sort of thing."

"I'm guessing Gideon didn't know where to find you, either. That's why he sent it to your friend Mike instead of to you directly?"

"Gideon must have figured that was the best way to get it to me. He did it before, sent a letter to Bryant to give to me. Bryant must have told him he had."

Bryant must have? "Why didn't you tell him?"

"I haven't spoken to Gideon in a long time."

"How long?"

He swallowed. "Not since that morning," he said roughly.

It took her a moment to realize which morning he meant—the only morning he could mean. There was only one night that had loomed so large in their thoughts for the past few days, and one morning after. It wasn't a lack of understanding that kept her from responding right away. It was shock. "You haven't seen him since your parents died?"

"No. Gideon managed to track me down a few years ago through Bryant. We were in the Army together. He must have tracked down everybody I served with until he found the one I still keep in touch with. It's the only way." He shook his head as if he still couldn't believe it.

The only one he kept in touch with, but not so closely that the man knew how to reach him or so often that months wouldn't pass before a wedding invitation got to him? So many questions she wanted to ask, but so many others that seemed more important. "Did you write back?" she asked when he didn't elaborate, even though she already knew the answer.

"No. I couldn't."

"Why not?"

Again, he didn't say anything for a long time, except this time she saw the shudder roll through his body, shaking his shoulders. When he did speak, she barely heard him, his voice a hoarse rasp.

"Because it was my fault."

More than the words themselves, it was the pain in them—bottomless, agonizing—that sent a chill through her. This time it was she who trembled.

"What was?" she asked just as softly, even though she once again knew what he had to be referring to, the only thing he possibly could, even if it made no sense to her.

He finally lifted his head and looked at her. What

she'd heard in his voice couldn't begin to compare to what she saw in his eyes. It struck her like a massive ocean wave crashing into her, freezing her to the core. She couldn't even swallow past the hard knot that suddenly formed in her throat.

Pain. So much pain.

"I left the door open."

The words were quiet, rough, barely spoken at all. They were still unmistakable in the utter stillness of the room.

She began to frown, to shake her head, to ask for an explanation.

It wasn't necessary. His gaze drifted away and he started speaking again almost instantly.

"Everybody thought there were four boys at home that night, because there were supposed to be. Gideon was staying over at a friend's, but everybody else was supposed to be home. Except they weren't."

"*I* wasn't."

"So where were you?"

"At Nate's house. That's Chief Cassidy, though obviously he wasn't back then. He was my best friend when I was a kid. He had this treehouse in his backyard where we used to spend all our time. We wanted to camp out that night. It didn't seem fair that Gideon got to spend the night with a friend on a school night and I didn't. It didn't matter that they were working on some school project and had to get there early the next morning. I just knew that if Gideon got to stay with a friend, I wanted to, too.

"I asked my mother. She said no, wouldn't even

think about it. I must have been a real pest, because
that's the closest I can remember her ever getting
to yelling at one of us. She said I was staying home
and that was it. It's stupid how mad at her I was. I
decided she couldn't keep me there if I didn't want
to be. I shared a room with Gideon and he wasn't
there, so nobody would know if I left. So I waited
until everybody was asleep, and when I thought it
was safe, I went out the back door.

"I didn't have a key. Teri used to bring us home
and she had a key, so there was never any need for
any of us to have one. I couldn't lock it if I wanted to
get back in the next morning without anyone noticing. So I didn't.

"I left the door unlocked."

*Sam knew he was still speaking. As though from
far away, he could still feel his lips moving, still
feel the rumble in his throat that indicated sounds
were being made and emerging from it. He heard
none of the words, the memories too vivid, as though
he'd been plunged into the past and was living it all
again.*

*He was lying in his bed, all alone in the room. He
heard the door open, felt his mom looking in the way
she always did. She seemed to linger longer than
usual this time, or maybe it just seemed that way
because he was so eager for her to go so he could
leave. He held his breath, waiting for it. Finally, the
door closed and she was gone.*

He saw himself sneaking out of the house, not

even thinking about what he was doing as he eased the door shut behind him without flipping the lock on the knob to latch behind him. Not thinking about the consequences or what could happen. As soon as the still-unlocked door was shut, he'd taken off across the yard, racing through the darkness to Nate's house.

He remembered waking that morning to the sound of birds chirping, Nate still asleep in the sleeping bag next to him. It wasn't even dawn yet, but he knew he had to get home. But first he'd lain there for a second and smiled, thinking how he'd gotten away with it and no one would ever know it.

He'd nudged Nate awake so he could get back inside his house and headed home. Nate lived a few streets over, so it was only a five to ten minute walk. Before he knew it, he was pushing through the trees into his backyard.

He was halfway across the yard when he heard the first scream.

He'd paused in midstep, his head jerking up, his heart jumping into his throat. The scream was quickly followed by another, then another, each loud and terrifying, all of them coming from inside the house.

In an instant, he took off for the house, running toward that closed door, reaching for the knob, knowing before he touched it that he wouldn't need a key.

The doorknob turned in his hand. He threw the door open, immediately recognizing the voice.

It was Josh.

Josh was screaming.

Then Sam saw him. He was kneeling on the floor between the sink and the center island. And on the floor in front of him—

He stopped breathing, shock squeezing his lungs until it felt like he was choking. It was his mom. His mom was on the floor. She was covered in blood. Josh was holding something to her stomach, pressing down, his own hands coated with blood.

"Mom?" he'd started to say, the word barely audible, even though some deep instinct recognized she wouldn't hear him anyway. She stared at the ceiling, eyes wide-open and unmoving. She was so frighteningly still, the only motions coming from Josh pushing against her stomach, trying to stop the bleeding.

Josh barely registered his presence, probably never noticed where he'd come from. He just kept screaming for help, for someone to come, for her not to die.

Mom, please! Please don't die! Pleasedon'tdie pleasedon'tdiepleasedon'tdie! Help, somebody! Somebody, please!

Help. The word broke through Sam's terror. He knew who could help, he knew who could fix this.

His dad. He had to get his dad.

He bolted for the hallway, screaming for his dad to get up. He pounded up those stairs, yelling at the top of his lungs the whole way. All he had to do was get his dad. His dad would know what to do. His dad would make it right again.

When he reached the upstairs hallway, he saw two little faces, staring at him wide-eyed from the door of their room.

"Get back inside and close the door!" he screamed.

Luke, the youngest, reached for Jake's hand, and Jake, who was too big to take it half the time, took it without question.

An image he'd seen for no more than a split second that had been burned so firmly into his memory banks the moment might as well have lasted for years.

He didn't stop to see if they obeyed. He tore down the hallway and burst into his parents' room, searching for help, for his dad, for someone who could fix this and make it right again.

Only to find more blood, more horror.

He skidded to a stop at the side of the bed, choking on the scream he'd been about to utter, the bile replacing it in his throat. The first rays of sunlight shone through the side window, illuminating the grisly scene.

His dad, the biggest man he'd ever known, lying there on his back with his eyes closed, like he was still sleeping. Except the front of his shirt and all the sheets were covered in blood, so much that it looked like he was sleeping on red sheets instead of white ones. So much that Sam didn't even have to touch him to know that he was dead.

The only person who could make everything right again was broken, too. He didn't know what to do. He didn't know what had happened. He didn't know what would happen now.

He'd only known one thing, the knowledge slowly falling over him as he stood there frozen, the words roaring in his ears, deafening him. The knowledge that remained with him to this day.

You did this. You left the door open.

This is your fault.

All your fault.

MAGGIE could feel the tears in her eyes at Sam's story, mirroring the ones sliding rapidly down his flat, lean cheeks. He didn't react to them. He simply stood there, staring blankly, lost in his own memories, reciting the story in a flat, unaffected tone that did nothing to rob it of its impact. It didn't matter. The look in his eyes related the horror of his tale so vividly she could almost see it herself.

When he was finally finished, he fell silent. Maggie struggled for something to say.

"That's why you were so sure Paul Winslow wasn't the killer simply because he had access to his daughter's key," she whispered.

"The killer didn't need one. Because of me."

"You can't really blame your—" She swallowed the rest of the sentence, aware even as she said it how foolish it was. Because it was obvious he did blame himself.

"You were just a kid. You didn't know what you were doing."

"It doesn't matter. I still did it. The result is the same."

That at least was one honest thing he'd told her. He'd said the killer had found some other way to get in. He just hadn't explained how he knew that was the case.

In fact, he still hadn't, she realized. It wasn't the only possibility. "You don't know that. There's still the possibility that Emily—that your mother opened the door."

"She wouldn't have opened the door in the middle of the night to just anyone. Besides, what are the chances she just happened to let in a killer on the same night the door was left unlocked?"

All right, so it might be slightly far-fetched. She decided to leave it be for the moment. Clearly she wasn't going to change his mind. He'd believed he was at fault for thirty years. She wasn't going to convince him otherwise without some effort.

Then it struck her. She stared at him, eyes widening. "You really haven't seen your brothers in thirty years?"

He shook his head sharply. "No. I can't."

"Why not?"

"How can I face them, knowing what I did? Knowing that I'm the reason our parents were murdered?"

And here they were again. Evidently it wasn't going to be escaped that easily. "If somebody came to the house in the middle of the night intending to hurt your parents, they weren't going to be turned away by a locked door. They would have found a way in even if the door was locked."

"But they didn't have to. If they'd broken in, they might have made a sound that would have woken somebody, warned them. Instead, the killer was able to get in without a problem, and there was no warning. Because of me."

"It's been thirty years. Even if it was your fault— which I don't believe it was—I can't believe your parents or your brothers would want you to punish yourself this long. They loved you. Clearly at least one of your brothers still does. If they actually did blame you, they would have forgiven you by now. You need to forgive yourself. You need to move on."

He finally met her eyes, shooting her a pointed look. "Really? *You're* going to talk to me about moving on?"

Heat flooded her cheeks. He was right, of course. She wasn't deluded enough not to recognize it. That didn't mean she wanted to hear it. And for a moment, she hated him a little for saying it.

She raised her chin and stared him down. "Yeah," she said. "Because if even I, of all people, know you need to move on, that should tell you something."

"It's not that easy." He sighed.

"I know," she said gently. "I definitely know that, too."

"That's why I'm here. I got the invitation and I

thought…maybe if I could find out who did it, maybe if I had the news to give them that the killer had finally been caught, then maybe I could go."

And he did want to go. He didn't have to say it. She could read the plain, open yearning on his face as well as if she were the one feeling it. She almost did, just looking at him, the need in his eyes striking her right at her very core.

Thirty years. He'd been alone, cut off from his family for thirty years. So many wasted years. And it had been long enough.

She swallowed the lump in her throat. "All right," she said. "Let's find out who did this."

He just looked at her, a heartbreaking combination of hope and disbelief flashing across his face. "You still want to?"

"Of course. Did you think I was going to stop just because I found out you lied to me? This person broke into my house, attacked me, set fire to the place. I'm not stopping now."

"Sure. I just didn't think—"

"That I'd want to work with you anymore? Well, I do," she said briskly, before he could even acknowledge the way she'd finished his comment. Things were different now, of course. Knowing the truth, knowing his reasons, didn't erase the fact that he'd deceived her. She wasn't sure she could entirely trust him again, and whatever dangerous closeness had formed between them was irrevocably broken. She felt its loss too keenly to believe otherwise. But that didn't mean she didn't want to help him. She still wanted the truth, and now she had even more reason. She wanted to make sure he saw his brothers again, not just for his sake, but for Greg and Emily Ross's.

When Irene had raised the likelihood that the boys had been separated, Maggie couldn't help but be affected by the tragedy that that represented, one tragedy on top of another. But to know that it had continued for thirty years… She could only imagine how their parents would feel if they knew.

She straightened her shoulders and met his eyes, doing her best to harden herself against the vulnerability in those eyes whose sadness she now understood too well. "Let's do this."

He looked at her for a long moment, with a trace of gratitude that threatened to crack her burgeoning resistance before it could fully form.

"Okay," he said finally, firmly. "Let's catch the killer."

Chapter Thirteen

"I can't believe you had a copy of the case file this whole time and didn't tell me," Maggie said as she pored over the documents he'd retrieved from his truck.

Sam sat on the adjacent side of the kitchen table, close enough to see the file, far enough to keep a reasonable distance. "I couldn't tell you."

"Only because you hadn't told me several other things you should have," she muttered. As much sympathy as she felt for his story, she wasn't going to let him off the hook for that one.

Wisely, Sam chose not to say anything to that. Sam… Strange how easily she'd come to think of him by his real name, almost as though she'd never known him by another. But then, it did seem to fit him better. For whatever reason, he did seem to be more of a Sam than a John.

She pushed the thought away to focus on the papers in front of her. "Have you already gone over this?" she asked.

"Not entirely. Nate gave it to me the night of the

break-in, and I only got to skim it. But it looks like Nate was right. The police questioned everyone they could think of, but with no firm evidence pointing to any one person, there was no way they could make an arrest."

He was right, she thought unhappily. Any hope that having the case file would make this easier had evaporated as soon as she saw the thin volume. The physical evidence was paltry. Of course, evidence techniques back then had been considerably less sophisticated than they were now, but even allowing for that, there just wasn't much there. No fingerprints had been found that shouldn't have been in the house. There were no signs of forced entry, as they already knew. The murder weapon was never found, though it was suspected to be one of the knives from the Rosses' own kitchen, one of the blades from the block on the counter being conspicuously missing. None of the neighbors had seen anything, none of the boys—the three who'd been home, she now knew— had seen or heard anything.

Emily Ross hadn't been completely dead when her son Josh found her, Maggie noted with a heavy heart. He said she'd still been blinking and moving her mouth slightly when he came down early and found her on the floor. Her husband had likely died quickly, the killer's stabs being exceedingly accurate. But he'd been asleep, a stationary target who hadn't been able to fight back. Emily Ross had likely been standing and alert when struck by her killer. There were only minimal defensive wounds on her body, possibly indicating she was caught by surprise by her attacker and unable to make more than a token attempt at defending herself. And whether it was the difficulty of killing a moving target or looking the victim in the eye, the wounds inflicted by her murderer hadn't been as deep or efficient. Her death had been a slow one, leaving enough time for her middle son to waken and come downstairs in time to witness her last breath.

Maggie shook her head, then shot a glance at Sam to see how he was reacting to the report. He wasn't looking directly at the paper, she realized, his jaw tense, his expression tight. She suspected he was just waiting for her to turn the page. Naturally, the gruesome details of his mother's death had to be hard for him to see.

For just a moment, she felt a burst of sympathy and nearly reached out to place her hand over his. She restrained herself at the last possible moment and instead used her fingers to simply turn the page.

In lieu of physical evidence, the police had questioned everyone possible. Anyone close to the Rosses who might have the slightest idea why someone would want to hurt them, anyone who might be considered an enemy who might have had a motive, however slight. Neither was a particularly long list. Most were the names she already knew, the suspect list being the same she and Sam had formed on their own.

All but one.

She froze at the sight of a familiar name she'd never considered. "Oh, my God."

Sam leaned closer. "What is it?"

"The police questioned Carl Graham about the murders. It doesn't say why, only 'because of his past history with the male victim.' Didn't you think that was significant when we talked to Irene?"

"Why would it be?"

She stared at him in disbelief. He only stared back at her, his brow furrowed, confusion in his eyes. Then it hit her.

"That's right," she said faintly. "I never told you Irene's last name." So it was her mistake, really. Just like trusting Irene in the first place had been.

"What is it?"

"Graham," she said. "Her last name is Graham. Carl Graham was Irene's husband."

You don't know that it means anything," Sam said with annoying level-headedness as he drove them to Irene's house. He'd insisted on driving, saying Maggie was in no mood to do so. Given the way she could barely sit still and felt on the verge of jumping out of her skin, she couldn't argue with him—at least about that.

"I know the fact that she didn't mention it sure as hell means something," she said. Instead, Irene had sat there and cast suspicion on everyone else she possibly could. It seemed so obvious now. Even in a town this size, the idea that a woman Irene's age would have been up on the high school gossip of people a decade younger was hard to believe. Yet Maggie had believed it. Because she wanted to, wanted to believe someone in this town would help her.

Because she was a fool, as her discovery about Sam had so thoroughly reminded her already today.

She pushed the thought aside, not wanting to pick at that particular wound any more at the moment. "I can't believe you're not angry about this."

"I've been angry with everyone since I set foot in this town," he said. "Knowing that all this time the killer was allowed to go free. Seeing how everyone seemed perfectly happy to have forgotten my parents. Seeing how they treat you."

She shot him a wry glance. "Nice try. If you're hoping to get on my good side, you've got a long way to go."

"I mean it."

"Maybe you do, but it's going to be a while before I start believing you mean what you say."

"Maggie," he said simply, softly, so much so that she was compelled to look at him. He glanced at her, his expression serious. "I am sorry. I never meant to hurt you."

For just a moment, the tenderness in his voice nearly softened her anger. And despite her words, she did believe him. But regardless of his intentions, he had hurt her. The humiliation was still too fresh to be forgotten so soon. "Fine. You didn't mean to hurt me. And maybe someday I'll care. Just not today."

After a moment, he nodded his acceptance and turned his attention back to the road. Maggie was glad he'd dropped it.

Suddenly, they were pulling into Irene's driveway. She hadn't called ahead, wanting to catch the woman by surprise. She had a feeling that that had been her mistake the first time. She'd given Irene time to think about why they would come to see her—no doubt an easy guess if she'd heard they'd both been researching stories at the library—and plan what she was going to say. It was a mistake Maggie had no intention of repeating.

Indeed, when Irene opened the door in response to Maggie's insistent knock, the woman appeared gratifyingly surprised to see them. "Maggie? What on earth is wrong?"

"We need to talk to you. Now."

Without waiting for an invitation, she brushed past Irene and stepped inside. Maybe it was rude, but certainly no more so than covering for a potential murderer.

Sam followed her in. From her expression, Irene wasn't sure whether to order them out or simply close the door and try to play a grudgingly gracious hostess. With obvious reluctance she finally closed the door.

As soon as she turned around again, Maggie spoke. "Why didn't you tell me your husband was questioned in connection with the Ross murders?"

The color draining from her face, Irene sucked in

a breath through clenched teeth. "How did you hear about that?"

"It doesn't matter. The only thing that does is the fact that you sat there and looked us both in the eye, casting suspicion on everyone possible while leaving out the fact that your own husband was a suspect."

"It wasn't relevant. And he wasn't a suspect. He was questioned once, and only then because the police were grasping at straws and questioning anyone with even the slightest motive, no matter how remote. After one brief conversation, they never spoke to him about it again."

"If it truly wasn't relevant, there was no reason not to get it out in the open, admit to it and get it out of the way. You had to know it would look suspicious if we found out on our own, so you sent us chasing after a half dozen other leads instead."

"I didn't think anyone else would even remember," the woman murmured, sounding every bit like she'd hoped that would be the case.

"Come on, Irene," Maggie scoffed. "You told us yourself you've lived here your entire life. Surely, you of all people know just how long this town's memory is."

Irene exhaled sharply. "Oh, believe me, Maggie, I know just how painfully long this town's memory is. Carl never would have been questioned in connection to the murders if that wasn't the case."

"So why was he?"

Looking every bit of her seventy-plus years, Irene dragged a hand over her face, stopping when her palm reached her mouth, as though she could hold the words in. Finally, when Maggie was about to press her further, she dropped the hand and sighed. "I told you that Greg Ross was in an accident that prevented him from playing college football." Maggie nodded. "He was out running one morning on the streets on the edge of town when he was struck by a car. A drunk driver coming home from a bar out by the highway early in the morning."

"Carl?" Maggie asked, trying to reconcile the image of a reckless drunk driver with her memories of Annie's father. She didn't remember much about him, only that he'd been nice enough to her. She couldn't recall his ever drinking, not that such a thing was likely to have stood out to her as a child. Of course, if he had injured Greg Ross while drunk, there may have been good reason why he wasn't drinking anymore at the time she'd known him.

"Carl used to have a drinking problem," Irene confirmed. "Back in the early days of our marriage. I almost left him over it. He was young and reckless, wouldn't come home until morning, having slept in his car because he couldn't figure out how to get home. If only he had slept it off a little longer that morning." She shuddered. "He felt terrible about what happened. It changed him. He pulled himself together after that, stopped drinking entirely and eventually we had Annie."

"So why would the police consider Carl a suspect? If anything, it sounds like Greg Ross had more of a reason to keep a grudge than Carl did."

"Because of the way people used to treat Carl after what happened, even after he got sober. Everyone might have been able to forget who he used to be if it wasn't for Greg Ross. He was a living reminder of what Carl had done. All you had to do was see Greg Ross and remember how he was supposed to be the best thing this town ever produced, and then remember why he never had the chance to live up to his potential. Because of my Carl and what he did. It was hard for him to get a job, even after years of sobriety and everyone knowing he wasn't drinking. Greg Ross had a lot of friends and even if he never told people not to hire Carl, he didn't have to. A lot of people would think they were being disloyal to Greg Ross if they did. Everybody knew Greg never really forgave Carl for what happened. It was only after he was killed and wasn't around every day to remind people that Carl really got a second chance around here."

"And maybe Carl knew that," Maggie deduced. "Maybe he'd had enough and realized the only way he'd get a fresh start was if Greg Ross wasn't around anymore."

"That's what the police considered. The idea is as ridiculous now as it was then. Besides, he was with me all night. Carl told the police, I confirmed it to them, and they left us alone after that."

"You lied for your husband yesterday. Who's to say you wouldn't lie for him back then?"

"I didn't lie yesterday."

"Believe me, lies of omission count," Maggie said. She was an expert on that point by now.

Irene didn't get a chance to respond. Another voice cut through the air from behind them. "My father wouldn't murder anybody."

At the sound of that voice, Maggie almost felt her heart crack in two. She'd hoped it wouldn't be true. But there was no denying it now.

Maggie turned to see Annie standing there, clearly having emerged from the kitchen. As Maggie's eyes met hers, Annie looked as wary as she damn well should.

Maggie pinned her with a glare. "You knew about this, didn't you?"

"Not at the time," Annie said. "I knew my father didn't drink, but I didn't know about his connection to the Rosses. My mother only told me once you came back and started working on the house. She was so worried people would start talking again, would start remembering that one mistake my father made rather than all the good things he'd done in the last twenty-five years of his life."

"So that's why you didn't approve of me fixing up the house."

"Only in part," Annie said, her eyes pleading. "I meant everything I said. I really don't think anyone's ever going to want to live there, and I don't think it's healthy for you, either."

"So you were thinking of me, and not just your own family's interests."

"Of course."

"I wish I could believe you." She wished she could believe anything anymore. Evidently she couldn't.

Suddenly she just wanted to get out of this house and away from these people. At the moment she actually wouldn't mind getting in the truck and not stopping until she was out of this town and away from its madness entirely. She'd just settle for leaving this house for now.

She looked up to see Sam watching her solemnly, concern darkening his eyes. "I think we're done here," she told him.

He nodded, and as she moved toward the door, she felt him follow.

"Maggie."

She was tempted to keep walking, but stopped nonetheless and looked back.

"My father's dead," Annie said. "There's no point in bringing any of that up and reminding people now. What are you going to do?"

"I don't know," Maggie said simply, the words not coming close to conveying the truth within them. "I just don't know anymore."

Ignoring the stricken look on Annie's face, painfully aware that anything her former friend was feeling was a pale shadow of the sorrow in her own heart, Maggie turned and walked away.

MAGGIE didn't say anything after they left Irene's house and started the drive back to hers. She stared straight ahead, her expression blank. Sam glanced at her out of the corner of his eye, but he couldn't tell what she was thinking.

Finally, when the silence had gone on too long, he forced himself to speak. "Are you okay?"

After a moment, she slowly shook her head. "I was just wondering if anybody is what they appear to be anymore. I guess you're the wrong person to ask about that, huh?"

He grimaced. "Sorry."

She waved off the comment. "I shouldn't have brought it up again. That's practically old news at this point." She sighed. "I was also thinking I might owe my mother an apology. I always thought she hated small towns. I might have misjudged her. Maybe she just hated this one." She exhaled sharply. "Suddenly I understand the feeling."

He opened his mouth to respond.

He never got the chance.

The jolt came out of nowhere, lurching through the truck, sending him crashing against the hard restraint of his seat belt. The air was knocked from his lungs. Beside him Maggie made a muffled sound of pain.

Blinking to clear his head, he glanced up in the rearview mirror. He started to ask Maggie if she was okay. The words died as soon as he saw the car behind them, accelerating fast for what had to be a second hit.

"Hold on!" he yelled. The words were nearly drowned out by the sound of the impact. He didn't have time to brace himself, the collision throwing him against the seat belt again. He slammed on the accelerator, trying to throw their pursuer. The other car remained behind them, having fallen back after hitting them, no doubt gearing up for another blow.

"What the hell is he doing?" Maggie asked.

"Nothing good," Sam grunted. As soon as he said it, the other vehicle started forward again with a roar of its engine. The second it did, he yanked the wheel, sending them to the left, then right. The other car tried to follow, weaving around the road behind them.

Sam eyed the street before them. This was a pretty open stretch of road between the neighborhood they'd just left and the one where they were headed. There was no other traffic, no other cars to worry about as he tried to escape the one behind them. Sam kept the truck moving across the lanes, trying to give the car a moving target that would be harder to hit.

"Can you see who it is?" he asked.

"No," Maggie said. "It's too bright. The sun's hitting the windshield just right."

He'd just pulled back into the right lane, the car behind them in the left, when the other driver seemed to lose patience with the game. Maybe he recognized it wouldn't be long until they reached a more heavily trafficked street and he wouldn't have them all to himself. Maybe he just was sick of not hitting them. The car pulled up beside them, halfway up the truck's body length, and rammed them from the side.

The backside of the truck fishtailed to the right, tires crunching on the gravel alongside the road. It was the worst possible position. Sam struggled to regain control, to get the truck straightened and moving forward again.

He didn't make it. The car hit them almost head-on in the side, slamming into the truck right behind Sam's door and driving them straight off the road.

The truck skidded, tires screeching, trying to gain purchase. Then kept moving, the vehicle lurching, dipping, as the tires went past the edge of the ditch lining the road.

In the split second before it happened, Sam threw an arm out, instinctively trying to hold Maggie back in her seat.

The truck fell on its side, then kept on going, teetering dangerously like it was going to flip over completely. Sam held his breath, braced himself, waiting for it to happen.

It didn't. With a groan, the truck flopped back over onto its side. It didn't move again.

Sam automatically looked to his right, where Maggie was, the side the truck had landed on. His heart thudding in his throat, it took him a moment to find his voice. "Are you okay?"

Breathing hard, she slowly turned her head to look up at him. "Fine," she muttered. "You?"

"Yeah," he said.

He watched her turn and check her surroundings. The ground pressed up against her window. The dirt and dust hovering in a cloud outside the windshield.

Beneath the hood, the engine ticked and shuddered ominously.

After a long moment, she glanced back at him, her eyebrows going up.

"I hate to say it, but I think your friend Mike is going to regret lending you his truck after all."

Chapter Fourteen

This time it was only ten minutes before Nate and one of his officers arrived on the scene. Evidently the accident had been harder for someone to ignore than the fire. Either that, or whoever called it in hadn't known who was involved. If they had, they may not have bothered reporting it, either.

"You sure you two are okay?" Nate asked after taking their statements.

"A little banged up, but we survived," Sam said. "That's the important part."

"Are you going to try to convince us this wasn't deliberate?" Maggie asked. She still sounded as irritated with Nate as she had from the moment they'd told him she knew the truth of Sam's identity, which he'd obviously played a part in keeping from her.

"No," Nate said sadly. "I don't believe for a second this wasn't intended to hurt you both. The good news is, this'll be a lot harder to hide than involvement in a fire. There aren't too many places in a town this size where a car with significant damage can be fixed—or hidden."

"Evidence," Maggie said. "Finally."

"I'll have the truck towed back to the garage. Can I drop you off somewhere?"

Sam glanced up and realized dusk was already beginning to fall. So much had happened today, it had passed incredibly fast. "Back to the motel, I guess."

Maggie shook her head. "It's going to be night soon. We have to get back to the house. Something could happen."

"Something *did* happen. We could have been killed. We've both been banged up. You need to rest, and staying up all night camping out on the floor of that house in case somebody shows up is not the way to do that."

"If this proves anything, it's that whoever is doing this is getting more and more desperate. There's no telling what they're going to do next. For all we know, they could be at the house now."

"It's just a house!"

"It's still worth saving!"

"Not as much as your life!"

Nate cleared his throat, breaking into the argument. "If I had to guess, whoever ran you off the road is going to be a little busy covering up the damage to his car to worry about the house tonight."

"But you don't know that," Maggie said.

"No," he conceded. He sighed. "Fine. I'll have one of my guys stay outside your house tonight."

"I thought it wasn't in your budget," she pointed out.

"It's not. This one'll be coming out of my pocket. I figure I owe you that much."

"You don't have to do that, Nate—" Sam started.

"Yeah, I do," he said, meeting Sam's eyes. "It might just be a house, but I don't want this bastard winning any more than she does. Do you?"

"No," he admitted. "I don't."

"Fine. So it's settled."

Sam looked at Maggie. "Agreed?"

She hesitated, though for a second he thought he detected something that looked awfully like relief in her expression. "All right," she said. "Agreed."

He swallowed his own relief, knowing the battle had just begun. It had been hard enough to get her to agree just to leave the house for the night.

She definitely wasn't going to like what he had to say next.

By the time they reached the motel, Maggie was feeling every ache and pain from the accident. Not that she was going to admit as much to Sam. There was nothing serious, just more bumps and bruises to add to the ugly purple splotch on her side where the intruder had kicked her the other night.

Nate had dropped them back at the house after all, so she could pick up some things and drive her truck to the motel. She was glad to have something to change into, because the clothes she had on felt grimy after everything that had happened that day, coated with dust and dried perspiration from those terrifying moments in the truck. She was already looking forward to spending a nice long time in a hot shower.

Something she could have done at the house, she thought, hoping she hadn't made a mistake agreeing to come here. After going through so much, the idea of losing the house and letting their attacker get what he wanted was almost enough to send her flying back to the door to head back there.

With some effort, she managed to stay where she was. She was about to ask him if he wanted to use the bathroom first when Sam said, "That's it."

Puzzled, she turned toward him. He stood in front of the door, having just closed it behind them, his features locked in a serious expression. "What's it?"

"This is too dangerous. You need to back off the investigation."

"Are you going to?" she asked, already knowing the answer.

"No."

"Then why should I?"

He stalked closer. "Because it's not your fight."

She dropped her bag at her feet and moved toward him. "The hell it isn't! I'm the one who had somebody break into the house and shove me down the stairs. I was in the house when they set it on fire and in the truck when they ran into us, same as you."

"And none of those things would have happened if you hadn't been asking questions. If you stop, this maniac won't have any reason to come after you."

"Do you really think he'll believe I've stopped asking questions? I think we've gone past that."

"Then you can leave town."

"I'm not going anywhere."

He took another step toward her, face dark with frustration. "Damn it, Maggie, I don't want anything to happen to you."

"I don't want anything to happen to me, either, or to you."

He waved off the comment. "Don't worry about me."

Her eyes flared. "So you're supposed to worry about what happens to me and I'm not supposed to worry about you. What kind of sense does that make?"

"I can take care of myself."

She barely heard the words as she studied him, taking in the color deepening his cheeks, the way he didn't meet her eyes. "So can I. But we all need somebody to worry about us, to care. You know how much the idea that I didn't have anybody here who cared bothered me."

He didn't respond. She finally realized how close they'd come to one another, gradually moving nearer in the heat of the conversation. She saw the instant he realized it, too. They were now mere inches apart, the air between them crackling with a tension that changed and deepened into a different kind once they both noticed just how little space separated them. A single step from either of them—that was all it would take until there was no space between them at all. Until their bodies were pressed together.

Before she could think about it, she reached out and placed her hand on his chest. She immediately felt a tremor quake through him, but he didn't pull away. She didn't do anything else, just touched him, just left her hand there and felt the solid muscle, his heart pounding beneath her palm, gaining speed with each passing moment.

"When's the last time you had somebody who cared about you?" she asked gently, even as she was painfully afraid she knew the answer.

"It doesn't matter. I don't need anybody."

"I don't believe you. And it's too bad, because you have me."

His eyes tracked over her face, lingering at her mouth, his own working slightly. She knew what was about to happen. And this time she didn't step away.

Then his mouth was on hers, his hands locked on her arms, pulling her to him. His lips worked over hers expertly, tenderly, hungrily. She responded in kind, eager for each kiss, wanting more from them, needing them to last longer. His tongue plunged into her mouth, claiming it, teasing her tongue, coaxing it to respond. In the back of her mind, she registered just how long she'd been waiting for this kiss, so long it seemed as though she'd been deprived forever. And maybe she had been. Because she'd never been kissed like this, never been devoured so eagerly.

Never wanted so much more.

Even as she thought it, her fingers were reaching

down to the hem of his shirt and pulling it upward. She felt the muscles of his midsection flex and tremor as her fingertips grazed them, working the shirt up over his belly. At the same time, he was reaching for her shirt, as well, fumbling with the buttons to work them free.

He pulled his mouth away for a moment to focus on them, freeing her own. "I thought we were supposed to be resting," she said, breathless, wanting his mouth on hers again.

"So we'll go slow and gentle," he murmured, the words sending a delicious shiver of anticipation through her.

There was nothing slow about the way they went about shedding their clothes, tearing them off each other and tossing them aside with abandon. With each garment that vanished and each stretch of skin that was exposed, they moved faster, more frantically. She felt his eyes on her body, never took her gaze off his. His body was as taut and lean and beautiful as she remembered. The mere sight alone was again enough to set her heart pounding even faster.

She'd only ever been with one man in her entire life, thought she would only ever want to be.

She'd been wrong.

She wanted this man. She wanted to touch him. She wanted to feel him. She wanted to have him deep inside her and to wrap her legs around him and bring him in deeper still. And even as she thought it, she knew even that wouldn't be enough.

But it would be a start.

Maggie reached out and shoved his pants and boxers down with one push, freeing him. Then he was in her hand, big and hard and straining. With a groan, he withdrew from her touch, retrieving his pants just long enough to tug his wallet from the back pocket and pull something from it. She lay back on the bed as he covered himself. Within moments, he joined her, leaning over her, covering her with the whole of him.

She ran her hands along his body as he positioned himself between her legs, feeling those flat planes and ridged muscles beneath her fingertips, even as she felt those rough, calloused, undeniably masculine fingers of his on her soft flesh. His right hand moved up to cup the back of her head, drawing it upward, until she was peering up into those deep blue eyes. It was there she was looking, into the tenderness of his gaze, when he thrust into her, long and slow and deeply.

For a moment, he simply remained there, buried in her without moving, staring deeply into her eyes. There was something so achingly tender in the way he looked at her, something she might have described as loving if she hadn't known any better. His thumb stroked over her cheek with the softest of caresses. Then he lowered his lips to hers, claiming her mouth as thoroughly as he had the rest of her body.

Only then, when his mouth was on hers, their tongues dancing, sliding, against each other, did he begin to move his hips. As promised, he moved slowly, gently, withdrawing with painstaking deliberateness, then pushing in again, harder, deeper. Then again. Lost in the sensations created by his kiss, in the warm heat flooding her chest, she responded gradually, raising her hips to meet his thrusts, tensing her body to draw him into her. She ran her hands over his back, hesitating briefly when they encountered the knot of scars there, then continued. It didn't matter. They were part of him. And she wanted him. She wanted this.

Her climax built slowly, just like his thrusts, steadily gaining momentum, growing more and more with each passing moment, each kiss, each caress. And when she finally couldn't hold on anymore, he was right there with her, emptying himself into her with a groan against her mouth.

When they were both sated, he rolled off her and onto his side, pulling her against his chest.

"I think I like your idea of resting," she murmured.

She felt him chuckle. "Slow and gentle enough for you?"

"Every bit as promised. I can't wait to see what hard and fast is like."

"Hey, you're the boss," he said against her ear. She jabbed him in the belly with her elbow, drawing another chuckle from him. "Just let me know when you're ready."

She twisted in his arms to face him. "I'm ready."

And she pressed her mouth to his.

Chapter Fifteen

"Are you finally ready to get some rest?" Sam asked hours later, lying beside Maggie, facing her.

She smiled, her breathing still rapid and uneven from their most recent encounter. "Worn out, are you?"

"Can you blame me?"

"Not a bit." *Restful* was the last word she would use to describe the past few hours, and she didn't regret it for a moment.

And yet, for all the pleasures of those hours, she had to admit this might just be her favorite part, lying here with him. Even after those hours, she still couldn't get enough of him. The mere sight of him kept her heart pounding in her chest, his body lean and beautiful, his eyelids heavy with satisfaction as he gazed back at her. But more than that, she cherished the closeness, somehow more intimate than anything else they'd done. Neither of them had bothered to cover up, the sheets crumpled in a heap somewhere on the floor. And yet, she didn't feel self-conscious and neither, it seemed, did he. It felt comfortable, easy, lying here, being with him.

His arm was slung over her. She trailed her hand over his side, still unable to get enough of touching him. As she did, her fingertips grazed something on his back. She didn't have to be able to see it to know what it was, and her heart lurched at the memory. "How did you get the scars on your back?" she asked softly.

He hesitated, then answered, "A punishment. One of the foster fathers was heavy into discipline."

"What did you do?"

"I got my parents killed."

She flinched. "He told you that?"

He shook his head. "I don't remember what he thought the punishment was for, but I knew why I deserved it."

Those scars hadn't been caused by a single incident, or even two. They'd been carved into his back over time. She could only imagine just how much time, and how much pain he'd endured. "Didn't you fight back?"

"No. Like I said, I deserved it."

"So you just let him hurt you?"

"It wasn't that bad," he said dismissively, though there was enough in his tone to indicate he was aware what a ridiculous lie it was.

"I'm sorry you went through that. You said one of the foster fathers. I take it there was more than one?"

"More than I can count."

"Did you ever find a permanent family?"

"No. I wasn't looking for one."

"If you say you didn't deserve one, I'm going to scream."

He didn't say it. He didn't say anything at all, the silence answer enough.

"What happened after you became an adult?"

"I joined the Army. Served a few years."

"And that's where you met your friend Mike," she concluded. "He certainly seems to think highly of you."

"He thinks I saved his life once."

"Did you?"

He just shrugged. Again, it was answer enough. If he hadn't, he would have said so. But being him, he wouldn't admit it if it were true.

"What made you leave the Army?" she asked, assuming he must have done so by choice since she hadn't seen anything to indicate he had any physical impairments that would preclude him from service. And she really couldn't imagine anything he could have done to get himself dismissed. A man carrying around as much guilt as he had wasn't going to do anything to add to it.

"You have to really want to be in the service to make a career of it. I didn't. I only joined because I didn't know what else to do. After a while it felt like my time was up, so I left."

"And then what did you do with the next, what, fifteen or twenty years?"

"Not much. Working. Getting by."

"You never got married? Never wanted to settle down?"

"I couldn't. You get close to somebody, they're going to expect to find out things about you. Who your family is. What your childhood was like. I couldn't tell anybody about that."

Running, she thought sadly. He'd spent all those years running from the past, until he'd finally come back to confront it.

"You never told anybody about that night?"

"No. Just you."

The significance of that hit her hard. "Why me?" she asked softly. "You could have just walked away. You didn't have to tell me."

He smiled. "You would have let me walk away?"

"No," she admitted. "The way I was feeling yesterday, I probably wouldn't. But you could have tried to talk your way out of it."

"Maybe. But I didn't want to. You deserved to know the truth. And I wanted you to know."

That cautious part in the back of her brain warned her not to take the words too much to heart. It was still too soon after learning the truth of his deception. She should know better than to believe anything he had to say.

Except she did believe him, knew it in her soul that he spoke the truth. After all they'd shared in the past day, after the newfound closeness that went far beyond anything they'd had before, she felt like she did know him, knew how to tell when he was being honest with her. And he was.

For whatever reason, he'd wanted her, more than anyone else he'd ever known, to know the truth.

As she heard his breathing steady and slow and knew he was falling asleep, she tried not to read too much into the comment, tried not to wonder what made her different. Even after everything they'd shared tonight, it would be foolish to put too much significance into whatever there was between them. She of all people should know better than to expect too much from anyone.

But as she drifted to sleep herself, she felt his arm tighten around her, and she couldn't help but acknowledge how good it felt to be with this man, and dream a little of what it would be like to stay that way.

THE next morning, after a shower that had proven longer than expected, they were finally planning to leave the room in search of food when there was a knock on the door.

It was Nate. If he noticed anything different between the two of them, he didn't comment on it.

"I've got news," he said without preamble. "Several people spotted Clay Howell driving through town with significant damage to the front of his car a short time after you were driven off the road."

So it was him after all, Maggie thought with a nod. She shouldn't be surprised, having seen the man's anger up close and personal. She glanced at Sam to see his reaction. Other than the tightening of his jaw, there was none.

"So you have the car?" Sam asked.

"Not yet. He must still be in it. I went by his house this morning. He's not home and his car's not in the garage. I'm about to go talk to Janet to see if she might have any idea where he'd go."

"I'll come with you," Sam said.

"*We'll* come with you," Maggie corrected.

Sam glanced at her like he wanted to argue, then simply sighed. The corner of his mouth curved in a hint of a smile. "We'll be right behind you, Nate."

Maggie didn't see Nate's reaction. She was too busy smiling back.

UNLIKE Sam, Maggie had never met Janet Howell. Her first impression of her was of a middle-aged, black-haired woman who appeared startled to find the three of them on her doorstep. As her gaze skimmed over Sam, Maggie had the impression the woman was on the verge of slamming the door shut. Then she caught sight of Nate, her eyes widening further.

"Can I help you?" she asked in a haltering voice.

"Mrs. Howell, I'm looking for Clay," Nate said. "He's not at home, and I have reason to believe you may be aware of his whereabouts."

"We're not married anymore. I don't keep tabs on Clay."

"But I've been informed you keep in close contact. When Mr. Samuels here paid you a visit, you wasted no time contacting Clay to let him know."

"He was looking for Clay. I thought Clay should know."

"And yet you told Mr. Samuels you didn't know where he was, the same way you're doing with me. Why should I believe you now?"

"Because I'm telling you the truth. I really don't know where Clay is."

"Mrs. Howell, this is serious. We're talking about attempted murder here."

She blanched. "What are you talking about?"

"We believe Clay drove these two off the road yesterday afternoon. They could have been killed or seriously injured, which we have to assume was his intention. Do you have any idea why he would have done that?"

Maggie had no doubt the woman knew exactly why. Janet closed her eyes and cringed, pain flashing across her face. "You might as well come in," she said faintly. "I think I need to sit down for this." She turned and retreated into the house, leaving them to follow.

They trailed her into a small living room. Janet sank into an armchair, not offering them seats. They found their own, Nate on the end of the couch closest to her, Maggie in another chair. Sam remained standing.

Janet's eyes went to him. "I knew this day would come. As soon as you came around asking questions." She looked at Maggie. "And you, with that house."

"You knew Clay would try to kill us?" Sam asked flatly.

"No. I knew I'd finally have to tell what happened that night."

Once again, there was no need to clarify which night was meant. "What did happen that night?" Nate asked.

She drew a breath. "Clay was supposed to be out of town."

"'Supposed to,'" Nate echoed. "So he wasn't?"

"No. He left, but he came back suddenly that night. I don't remember why. Maybe leaving town at all was nothing more than a ploy to catch me, because he knew."

"Knew what?"

She opened her mouth, but it took several moments before any sounds came out, as she sucked in and released a long, ragged breath.

"I was having an affair," she finally whispered.

"With whom?"

She gave her head a vigorous shake. "I'm not going to tell you that. It doesn't matter. The only thing that does is that Clay thought it was with Greg Ross."

"Why?"

She barked out a laugh, the noise bitter and humorless. "Because he thought everything was about Greg Ross. He didn't even want me to work for Dalton because Greg did. Ever since high school, it was like he was obsessed with the man. He always wanted to be better than him, always wanted to beat him, when I'm pretty sure Greg didn't give him a second thought. Come to think of it, Clay must have known it, too, and I'm sure that only made him madder.

"When he came home that night, I was getting dressed up in a way that obviously indicated I was going out with a man. He stood there in the bedroom doorway and he said, 'I knew it. You're sleeping with somebody. Who is it? Greg Ross?'" She threw her hands up. "My God, I was so tired of hearing about Greg Ross. I still am. So I told him, 'Maybe I am. Maybe—'" she sucked in another breath "'—maybe if you were any kind of real man instead of an insecure child, I wouldn't have to.'

"He started screaming about how stupid I was, that Greg hadn't wanted me in high school, that I was fooling myself if I thought he would ever leave Emily for me." She snorted. "Like I didn't know that. I wasn't interested in hearing any more, so I left. I went to meet the man I was seeing exactly as planned. We spent the night together at a motel, and I tried to forget all about Clay.

"The next morning I came home. Clay was here. He was sitting right here in this room, and he looked terrible. He was wet, like he'd taken a shower, but I could smell the liquor on him. He just stared at me with this awful look in his eyes, then he stood up and walked out.

"And then I heard that Greg and Emily Ross had been murdered, and I knew what he'd done."

"Did he ever tell you he did it?"

"No. He didn't have to. And I didn't ask. Because then I would have had to admit that it was my fault. If I hadn't said what I had—" She choked on a sob. "Those people. Those poor people."

"If you thought he was a killer, why didn't you turn him in?"

"Because he was my husband," she said simply. "I might not have been happy with him, but I couldn't be the one to send him to jail, especially when it was my fault. He never would have done what he did if I hadn't said what I did. And it wasn't just about me. If I'd told the story, I would have had to admit the affair, and the man I was involved with probably would have been exposed. I can only imagine how *he* would have reacted, having people know he was carrying on with a married woman."

"If you were dedicated enough to your husband to keep his secret, why did you divorce?"

"Because it became too much, living with it hanging there between us. We never talked about it. We didn't have to. It was always there, the elephant in the room. I knew the only way I'd ever have a chance of forgetting was to not have to face Clay across the kitchen table every day."

"Mrs. Howell, I'm going to have to ask you again, do you have any idea where Clay might have gone?"

She didn't say anything for a long moment. Maggie

couldn't tell if she was stalling or simply thinking, but Janet finally opened her mouth and said roughly, "My father had a fishing cabin out by the lake. Clay still has a key."

"Thank you. I'm going to have to ask you not to call him and warn him we're on our way."

"I won't. There's no point anymore, now is there? The truth is out. I don't have to cover for Clay anymore."

If she was relieved by the idea, it didn't show. She simply looked defeated, sinking back in her chair as a single tear fell down her cheek.

"OKAY," Nate said as they left Janet Howell's house. "This is the end of the line for you two. I'll give you a call once Howell is in custody."

"I'm coming with you," Sam said.

"No, you're not," Nate replied automatically, at the same time Maggie said, "What are you talking about?"

"Yes, I am," Sam said, ignoring Maggie's comment. "I want to be there."

"I've given you enough allowances, Sam, but I have to stop here. Talking to Janet Howell is one thing, and frankly to my advantage, since it was harder for her to avoid Clay's actions when the two people he tried to kill were sitting right in front of her. But I'm looking to make an arrest and I don't need civilians in the way."

"I'll stay out of the way," Sam said with more stubbornness than she'd ever seen him display.

"It could be dangerous," Maggie said. "We have no idea how he'll react to being cornered. He could be armed."

"She's right," Nate said. "You should listen to her."

Sam finally looked at her. "After all this, you want to back down *now?*"

"Once again, that should tell you something."

"I came here to find out who killed my parents."

"And you've done that!"

"It's not enough! I want to be there. I want to see that bastard taken away. I need that. Can't you understand that?"

The plea was etched across his face as openly as in his words, and for a moment Maggie's resolve faltered. Despite the danger, despite knowing there was nothing they could contribute, she almost wanted to give this to him. Not the Sam she knew now. The Sam from thirty years ago. The Sam who'd found his parents killed and blamed himself and never known who committed the crime. She could see that boy in the man standing before her, the boy who needed to be there to see his parents' killer brought to justice.

But more than that, she needed to know that the man before her, the man she cared about to a frightening degree, wouldn't be hurt for no reason.

"I understand it," she said gently. "I just can't agree with it."

His shoulders heaving, Sam turned to the chief. "Come on, Nate. You can't leave me out of this now. You know I have to see this."

At first Maggie was sure Nate wouldn't be swayed. After all, it had been him to refuse in the first place.

But when she looked at Nate, she saw his resolve hadn't been as firm as her own. He seemed to waver before her very eyes, until he finally sighed and dropped his head, giving it a shake. When he looked up again, he pointed directly in Sam's face. "Okay, you stay in the car. Get in the way, and I'll arrest you, too."

Maggie could only stare at the man in disbelief, unable to believe what she was hearing. But then, maybe she shouldn't be surprised, she thought as she took in the look on his face. He'd known the boy Maggie could only imagine, and he'd clearly been affected by the Ross murders, too. Perhaps it was too much to expect him to deny an old friend such a request. It seemed none of them could escape the past.

"Agreed," Sam said. He turned his attention back to Maggie. He placed a hand on her arm. "It'll be fine. I'll be careful."

She just looked at him, dread gnawing at her insides, and tried to believe him, even if she couldn't come close.

Chapter Sixteen

After she returned to the house, Maggie tried to think about anything other than what Sam and Nate were up to. Terrifying visions of Clay Howell making his last stand kept flickering through her mind, bloody images of Sam caught in the crossfire. She almost wished she'd gone, too, but she'd meant what she said. There was nothing she could contribute. She didn't want to get in the way. And if something did happen to Sam, she wasn't entirely sure she could bear to see it.

Instead, she focused on the fire damage she still hadn't dealt with. Clay must have been terrified they'd figure it out to go to such trouble. It was hard to believe all of this had happened because of a lie. Two lives taken, five children orphaned, all because of one man's obsession with an old rival and a wife's affair.

She wondered idly who Janet's lover had been. It must be someone who was still in town and still alive, or someone who had family that was. Janet wouldn't still be worried about the man's identity being revealed if that wasn't the case. If it was the latter, it would be someone who hadn't had family at the time, or someone who'd been able to sneak away for a full night without difficulty. Strange how many people were away from home, or supposed to be, that particular night.

Unless it wasn't a coincidence.

And just like that, she knew.

She froze, considering the obviousness of it. Then, before she could stop herself, she hurried inside the house and called directory assistance. She wasn't entirely sure why. It hardly mattered at this point. But it was a loose end, and Maggie was sick to death of those.

Once she had the number she wanted, she dialed it. When there was no answer at first, she hung up and dialed again.

It took three tries, but Janet Howell finally answered. "Hello?"

"Mrs. Howell, this is Maggie Harper. Please don't hang up," she said quickly when she suspected the woman was on the verge of doing just that, then held her breath to see if she had.

"What do you want?" Janet said finally.

"The man you were having an affair with. It was Paul Winslow, wasn't it?"

The gasp that came across the line was confirmation enough before she said a single word. "How did you—" She stopped abruptly, silence echoing for several long moments. "Yes," she said, the word barely audible. "How did you know?"

"I spoke to his daughter a few days ago. She mentioned he was out of town the night of the murders, leaving her home alone. It seemed a little coincidental for so many people connected to the Rosses to be out of town that night, and I have to admit I've noticed some similarities between the two men, personality-wise," she said tactfully.

Janet laughed softly. "I did have a type, didn't I? Always the bad boy. Nice guys never gave me the time of day. Guys like Greg Ross." There was no bitterness in the words, only a faint trace of wistfulness, and perhaps pain.

"Why didn't you stay together after your divorce from Clay?"

It wasn't until the question was out that Maggie realized just how personal it was. Before she could apologize for any offense, Janet simply sighed. "We'd actually broken up before then. I wanted children, and I knew Paul wasn't the man I wanted to father them. As it was, he certainly wasn't much of a father to the child he already had. I didn't know he left Teri alone the nights we were together. He always said she was spending the night at a friend's house."

"Didn't you wonder why you had to go to a motel instead of his house?"

"One of his neighbors might have seen me, and then everyone would know. There aren't many secrets in Fremont."

Maggie bit her tongue rather than disagree. If there was one thing she'd learned the last several days, it was that there were plenty of secrets in Fremont.

Janet tsked softly. "That poor girl. To have a father like that, then to lose two teachers she was so close to one right after another like that."

Maggie frowned. "What do you mean *two* teachers?"

"Well, there was Emily Ross, of course. Then there was Spencer Barton. He was one of the most popular teachers at the high school. He was after my time. In fact, I think he was about my age. I just remember that after he died, all the kids got together to raise money for a plaque in his honor at the school."

Maggie suddenly remembered the plaque she'd seen at the high school. "What happened to him?"

"He died in a house fire. It must have been a little more than a year after the Rosses were killed. Such a tragedy. Obviously he meant a lot to all the kids there, but I remember he meant a great deal to Teri in particular. Paul said he was giving her some special tutoring. I remember because he seemed so happy about it, as though pleased someone else was taking an interest in her because he wouldn't have to."

Maggie barely heard most of the woman's comments, her mind stopping on the very first.

Spencer Barton had died in a house fire. Her own attacker seemed to have an inclination toward fire as a tool of destruction. Another strange coincidence?

Unless it wasn't a coincidence.

She needed more information, more than she suspected Janet Howell could provide. And she needed it now.

"Thank you, Mrs. Howell," she interrupted whatever Janet had been saying, her thoughts already far from the other woman. "You've been very helpful." Without waiting for a response, she disconnected the call.

She was already reaching for her keys before she lowered the phone.

Two officers were already waiting, their vehicles tucked out of sight of the fishing cabin, when Nate pulled up at the scene. Nate had called the station and ordered all available officers to meet him there. Sam had expected there to be more than two, but clearly he'd overestimated the size of the Fremont Police Department.

As soon as Nate's cruiser pulled to a stop, Sam opened his door.

"Hold it," Nate said. "I told you to stay in the car."

"We're far enough from the scene here, aren't we? I can't get in the way all the way back here." He climbed out before Nate could respond, hearing the other man swear before emerging himself.

The officers walked up to Nate, a welcome distraction taking his attention from Sam. "You're sure he's here?" Nate asked them.

The taller of the two nodded. "Looks that way. The car's parked out front, the damage clearly visible. Unless he walked out of here, he's still here."

The words had barely left his mouth when the

sound of hinges squeaking reached them, followed by muffled cursing.

Nate was already reaching for his weapon before he took off in that direction. "Stay here," he told Sam, not sparing a glance before he headed toward the cabin, his gun in his hands. The other officers trailed close behind.

Sam waited all of five seconds, until they disappeared around the bend, before following.

"Freeze, Howell," he heard Nate order.

Sam turned the corner in time to see Howell do just that. He was standing a few feet in front of a run-down cabin, looking scruffy and disheveled, his hair sticking up all over his head, his clothes wrinkled and creased like he'd slept in them.

From the looks of it, he was also drunk, as he demonstrated once he reeled back in surprise, the flailing of his limbs nearly taking him off his feet, and started to stumble back unevenly into the cabin. Nate and the officers were on top of him and had him in cuffs before he could even try to struggle. He could barely get his legs to work, let alone his arms to fight back, as they collapsed beneath him and he fell to the ground in a heap.

Sam slowly moved closer, unable to take his eyes off the man. To know that this was the person who'd killed his parents, had tried to kill him and Maggie… Rage exploded in his veins, and it was all he could do not to launch himself at the man.

"Clay Howell, you're under arrest for attempted

murder," Nate said. He began to recite the man's rights.

He only managed a few lines before the man interrupted. "I had to do it," he slurred. "He wouldn't leave Janet alone. They were going to figure out what she did. I had to protect her."

"What *she* did?" Nate repeated.

"It's all my fault. She never would have done it if I'd been a better husband."

"What did she do?" Sam said, drawing a glare from Nate he ignored.

"Killed 'em," he said, and then the man actually started to cry. "She killed 'em."

"Are you saying you think Janet killed Greg and Emily Ross?" Nate asked.

"She always did have a temper," Clay babbled. "He was never going to leave that wife of his. That's what I told her that night. She must have gone crazy after he told her. She didn't come home all night, and when she did, she looked all guilty. When I heard what happened, I knew. The way she looked at me, she was so scared, so scared because of what she did. I had to protect her, don't you see? I had to make up for not being a good enough husband to her."

The man began to sob in earnest, turning his mottled face even redder. Nate, Sam and the others just looked at each other in stunned silence.

Finally Nate shook his head. "We'll have to settle this back at the station." He gestured to the two officers. "Get him out of here."

Stunned by what he'd just heard, Sam barely

noticed the officers shuffling Howell back to their vehicle. He didn't even see Nate coming up to him until the man was right in front of him. "Hey."

"He didn't do it," Sam muttered. Hearing the words aloud, coming from his own mouth, did nothing to make them seem more real.

"He could be lying."

"He's too drunk to be lying. You smelled him just as well as I did. He's incapable of lying in the shape he's in. He means every word he's saying."

Nate nodded. "Most likely. I guess that means we need to go back and talk to Janet."

"She didn't do it. He might think she did—hell, it looks like they both really think the other did—but she didn't do it any more than he did."

"How do you know?"

"The only way Janet has a motive for the murders is if she really was having an affair with my father, and I don't believe that for a second. My dad wouldn't have cheated on my mom."

"I know you want to believe that, but you were just a kid. Kids never have a true picture of who their parents were."

"I'm telling you it's not possible."

"Sam, I'm just trying to be clear-headed about this."

"Well, don't," Sam snapped. "You're wasting your time—and mine."

He turned to head back to the car. He was halfway there when the magnitude of the revelations finally hit him, nearly stopping him in his tracks.

He'd failed. The wedding was in two days, and he was still no closer to learning the killer's identity.

He couldn't go.

Despite Maggie's reassurances, he knew it was true. He couldn't go there, couldn't look the others in the eye knowing what he'd done without having something to offer them.

Which meant he couldn't go.

The disappointment hit him all at once, all of it, learning that they hadn't found the killer after all, realizing he couldn't go to the wedding.

This time he did stop, struggled to pull himself together so he could keep moving, the way he'd always done.

It was all he could do. Keep moving forward, even if he didn't have anywhere to go, just so he didn't have to look back.

MAGGIE braced herself for Shelley Markham's dour scowl before she even opened the door to the library. It still didn't help completely dilute the effect as the woman aimed it at her as expected.

Ignoring it as much as possible, Maggie walked straight up to the front desk. "I need to look up information on a Spencer Barton. I'm told he died in a house fire about thirty years ago."

"I'm busy at the moment," the woman sniffed, even though it was clear she was no such thing.

Maggie forced a sickly sweet smile. "It won't take

but a moment of your time. I actually know the year. I just need to know around which date to look."

"As I said, I'm busy."

"Well, I'm not going anywhere. So I guess we can just stand here staring at one another until you decide to do your job and help me."

The corners of the woman's mouth turned up in a smirk. "I do believe you're creating a disturbance. If you don't leave, I'll call the police."

"The entire police department is rather busy at the moment. They're arresting the person who ran me off the road yesterday. I'm sure you've heard about that, just as I'm sure you've heard about all the things that have happened to me since I came back to town. Frankly, it's been a rough few days. And after everything I've been through, if you think a librarian with too much attitude is going to intimidate me, think again. Now when did the fire happen?"

The woman's eyes flared with outrage, her lips compressing to a line so thin it looked as if she'd swallowed them. For a moment, Maggie thought she still wasn't going to tell her.

Then the woman opened her mouth, her lips still nowhere in sight. "October," she said in a strangled voice. "It happened in October."

"Thank you." Maggie grinned, not even trying to keep the smugness from her face.

Mrs. Markham didn't fail to notice, her eyes narrowing to slits. "You don't belong in this town," she spat.

Maggie just laughed. "Well, thank God for that,"

she said, enjoying the way Shelley Markham's eyes widened in shock. "I know you think you're insulting me, but frankly that's the nicest thing anyone's said to me since I set foot in this town."

NATE didn't have one of his officers drop Sam off back at the house until late afternoon. He'd remained at the police station when they brought Janet Howell in for further questioning. As would be expected, she'd denied killing his parents or having an affair with his father. She'd revealed after only minor pressing that it was Paul Winslow she'd had an affair with, asking if Maggie hadn't already told them. At the reminder of Maggie, Sam realized he'd been away from her too long, and he had no interest wasting any more time with the Howells, two people who each believed the other was a murderer, neither of whom were, both of whom seemed to thoroughly deserve each other.

Lost in thought, Sam was already out of the police car before he noticed Maggie's truck wasn't in the driveway. He stood there for a moment, listening to the sound of the cruiser pulling away, and stared at the space where her truck should be. If she wasn't here, then where was she?

He could only assume she'd gone into town. It wasn't like there were so many places around here to go. He turned to ask the officer for a ride back into the heart of town, only to see the cruiser was too far down the street. There was no way he'd catch up with him.

With a sigh, he faced the house. The mechanic at the garage in town had left word at the station that his truck was good to go, but they'd already been closed by the time he'd gotten the message. Without a vehicle, there was nothing he could do but wait.

Trying not to let his usual uneasiness about the house get to him, he forced his feet to move forward, until he'd climbed the steps and stood at the front door.

Maggie had given him a key. He pulled it out of his pocket and unlocked the door, then sucked in a breath before pushing on the surface. It slowly squealed open, revealing the empty entryway, the rooms and corridors before him already beginning to grow long with shadows from the late-afternoon sun. That eerie stillness hung over the place, the quiet as unsettling as ever.

Stepping inside, he flipped the switch inside the door to turn on the light in the entryway and closed the door behind him. He knew too well he wasn't going to be able to sit still in the kitchen. Just the thought of it made his skin crawl.

Instead, he moved into the room to his right, the room that had been a living room when he'd lived here. He didn't have any bad memories of this room. In fact, they were mostly good. This hadn't been where his parents died, it had been where they'd lived. Where all of them had lived, the seven of them. He could almost see them here, hear them laughing, the way it had once been.

Suddenly he heard a sound behind him. Was there somebody here after all? It couldn't be Maggie; her truck was gone. He started to turn.

He didn't even make it halfway.

He never saw the hard object arcing toward his head, but he felt it, the blow blurring his vision and driving him to his knees.

Before he could recover, the weight slammed into his head again, knocking him to the floor.

His vision was already fading when he heard the footsteps approaching as though from a great distance, just before one final blow stole his consciousness completely.

IT was already growing dark by the time Maggie left the library. She could have printed the articles to take with her, but rather enjoyed getting Mrs. Markham's goat simply by being there, rubbing her nose in her presence.

Not to mention she'd been engrossed in them as soon as she'd started reading, too much so to worry about committing them to paper.

The stories had largely confirmed what Janet Howell had told her. Spencer Barton had been a very popular teacher at the high school, beloved by the student body. He'd been thirty-two and unmarried, and every single article had described him as handsome. He'd died in a fire one night at his home.

He'd been a smoker, and it was believed he must have failed to entirely extinguish a cigarette or fallen asleep with one still lit. He'd never even had a chance to escape.

On the surface, it was nothing like Emily Ross's death. Emily Ross had been murdered; Spencer Barton had died in an accident. Emily Ross had been stabbed to death; Spencer Barton had died in a fire. They had nothing in common except the fact that they were teachers at the same high school and they both were purportedly close to one student.

There was no reason to believe they were connected. Sam and Nate had gone to arrest the person most likely responsible for Greg and Emily Ross's murders.

But she couldn't shake the feeling that there was a connection, just as she had an uncomfortable suspicion she knew what it was. She simply didn't have enough pieces to see the whole picture.

The first thing she saw when she reached the house was that the lights were off. She assumed that meant Sam wasn't back yet. She frowned, thinking just how long it had been since he'd left with the chief. She wondered if he and Nate had managed to find Clay Howell, and if so, whether he'd confessed to the Ross murders. That would certainly put her nagging suspicions to rest.

But then, if they had found him and something had gone wrong, that would explain why Sam wasn't back yet, she thought with a sinking heart, her earlier concerns coming back with a vengeance. She swallowed, the images of Sam getting hurt returning to her mind, each worse than the last.

Of course, if he was in the kitchen, she wouldn't be able to see the lights from the front. In that case, he could have just not bothered turning on the lights in the main rooms.

Hoping that was the case, she hurried out of the truck and toward the house, his name on her lips as she reached for the doorknob. She pushed the door open.

"Sam?"

The word was barely out of her mouth when the smell hit her, the stench so strong it was unmistakable.

Gasoline.

She froze in the open doorway, fear washing over her, creating goose bumps on her skin. The light wasn't on in the kitchen, casting its comforting glow down the hallway. It was as she'd thought from outside. All the lights were off. All she could see were the shadows created by what little fading sunlight managed to break through the windows.

She hesitated on the threshold, unsure what to do. The only possible cause for that smell was if someone had dumped gasoline in the house, someone who'd done that for only one purpose. That purpose obviously hadn't been fulfilled, given that the house was not on fire.

Not yet anyway.

Which meant that the person who'd done it was still here.

It was all she could do not to rush into the house to try to save it, to find the person responsible and stop them before they could act. Some deep-seated preservation instinct held her in place, recognizing the foolishness of such an action. If the house did go up, it was unlikely she could do anything but go up with it.

So she stood there, trying to decide on her course of action. She listened carefully, seeking some sound to indicate the intruder's location. She scanned the shadows for the slightest clue, anything that shouldn't be there.

The glint of something metal caught her eye. She zeroed in on a spot on the floor to her right, just inside the entryway of the room. It took her a moment to make out the shape, to recognize what it was.

A key.

It was a single key on a small metal ring. Just like the one she'd given Sam.

Her heart lurched, then picked up speed. There was no reason for that key to be there unless Sam was, or had been here. He could have simply dropped it, although she had to believe he would have noticed it. The sound of the key hitting the hardwood floor would have been plainly noticeable in an empty room. And if he'd noticed it, he would have picked it up.

Unless he was unable to.

Possibilities flooded her mind, none of them good.

And she knew she had no choice but to walk into that house.

The house wasn't really worth risking her life for. But Sam was.

She wasted no time, quickly moving inside as soon as the knowledge struck her. She went straight to the key, picking it up. She knew immediately it was the same one she'd given Sam.

The smell of gasoline was so thick it threatened to suffocate her. Maggie raised her arm to her face, trying to breathe through the fabric of her shirt. Clutching the key in her hand like it was a lifeline leading her to Sam, she slowly moved forward through the room and into the next, walking on the balls of her feet to remain as quiet as possible. The rooms were heavy with silence.

And then she heard it. The familiar creak of a floorboard being stepped on.

Directly behind her.

She froze, waiting for whoever it was to say something, ready to lunge forward if she sensed them moving closer. Based on the sound, the person was at least a few feet away. Clearly they had to know she was aware of their presence based on her reaction. Just as clearly, it wasn't Sam or any other friendly party who would have no reason not to identify themselves.

No, this was an enemy, the one she'd been waiting for since the attacks on the house had first begun. It was as obvious as the stench of gasoline all around her.

When the person didn't say anything, Maggie knew it was going to be her move. She turned slowly, the greeting rising to her tongue even before she saw who was behind her. There was no need. She already knew.

"Hello, Teri."

Chapter Seventeen

Teri Winslow stared back at her, the gasoline can still clutched in her right hand. The expression on her face was oddly calm. It was more terrifying than if she'd been displaying outright anger. She simply looked at Maggie as though she hadn't been caught doing anything wrong.

"You know, don't you?" she said.

"That you killed the Rosses?" Maggie asked. "Yes, I know."

"Who else does?"

"As far as I know, just the police chief," Maggie lied. "Though he's probably told the rest of the department by now, and it might have gotten out from there."

"How did you figure it out?"

"The fire," Maggie said. "Spencer Barton died in a house fire. Somebody set fire to my house, the same person who seemed to be upset that I was investigating the murder of Emily Ross, who was a teacher at the high school with Spencer Barton. It seemed too much to be a coincidence."

With a nod of acceptance, Teri glanced down at the can in her hand. "Maybe I should have thought of that. But it worked so well before. I was hoping it would be as effective."

"At killing me?"

"No," Teri said softly. "At erasing mistakes."

"You killed Spencer Barton. He was the mistake you wanted to erase?"

Teri winced as though Maggie had struck her. "Yes," she said faintly.

"I admit I don't know why, just like I don't know the connection to Emily Ross, though I can probably guess. Part of me hopes I'm wrong."

Teri briefly closed her eyes. "You're not wrong," she whispered.

"There was something between you and Spencer Barton, something more than a student–teacher relationship?"

"We were lovers," Teri said bluntly. "I was fourteen when he seduced me. From then on, I was at his house every chance I had. It's not like my father was ever around to know. I was in love with him. I thought he loved me, too."

"Emily Ross found out, didn't she?"

"She saw us after school that day. Nothing too explicit, but enough that she had to know something was going on. Spence—he was leaning close, too close to be completely innocent. He was murmuring in my ear, and I was giggling. I remember looking up and seeing Mrs. Ross standing there. We both did. She didn't say anything. She just stood there, staring at us with this look on her face. We moved apart quickly, tried to act like there was nothing out of the ordinary between us, but we could both tell she was suspicious."

Yes, she had been, Maggie realized. And newly reminded of the dangers that lurked in the world, even in a small town, she'd gone home and tried to hold her children close to her that night, refusing to let her son make unexpected plans to stay at a friend's house.

That's the closest I can remember her ever getting to yelling at one of us. She said I was staying home and that was it.

"Spence lost it," Teri continued. "I'd never seen him so upset. He said she was going to ruin everything. She would tell the principal and he would be fired and have to leave. We were supposed to spend the night together because my father was out of town, but Spence was too upset. He made me go home.

"I stayed up all night. I couldn't sleep. I just kept thinking about how Mrs. Ross was going to tell and they were going to take him away from me and he was all I had. And finally I decided I couldn't let her take him away from me. I had to stop her. I didn't have anybody else."

"You had Emily Ross," Maggie couldn't help pointing out. "She cared about what happened to you, more than Spencer Barton ever did."

"I know that now. I didn't then. I thought—" She sucked in a shuddery breath and shrugged helplessly. "I thought he loved me."

A twinge of recognition struck Maggie at how lost the woman sounded. She nearly felt a hint of sympathy for her.

Then she thought about Greg and Emily Ross and their children.

And Sam.

"How did you get into the house?" she asked, figuring she knew the answer, hoping she was right.

"I came in the back door. I used my key."

"It was locked?"

Teri frowned. "Of course."

And there it was, the truth at long last. Greg or Emily Ross must have checked the door and locked it, after Sam left the house, before Teri arrived. All those years Sam had spent in guilt for no reason, when he truly never had been at fault at all.

"But why kill Greg Ross?"

"I didn't intend to. I didn't really think about him. I just knew I had to stop her. So I let myself in, took a knife from the kitchen and went up to their bedroom. Except she wasn't there. Only Mr. Ross was there, and I realized she might have told him. I couldn't let him tell, either. And then he started to wake up, and I panicked."

"Where was Emily Ross?"

"In the bathroom down the hall. I passed by her without even realizing she was in there. When I was…done with Mr. Ross I heard the bathroom door open and waited for her to come back. She didn't. She went downstairs to the kitchen. So I followed her."

"Did she see you?"

Teri swallowed, and when she spoke, Maggie could hear the tears in her voice. "Not at first. Not until right after I came up behind her. She turned around and I stabbed her. She didn't even say anything. She just stared at me, and I stabbed her as much as I could, just thinking about how she was going to take Spence away from me, until I couldn't take that look in her eyes anymore."

"Did Spencer Barton know what you'd done?"

"I never told him. And if he suspected, he never let on. He was just so relieved, and I was so happy that he was relieved and we could be together. I never let myself think about Mr. and Mrs. Ross or the kids."

"Then why did you kill him?"

"I went to see him that day after school. We weren't spending as much time together anymore. I didn't understand what was happening, I didn't know why. Then I looked through the window and saw him with another girl, a freshman. She couldn't have been more than fourteen. I was sixteen, a little long in the tooth for him, I guess. And then I saw him for what he really was. He didn't love me. He never had. He was just a garden-variety pervert who was into young girls. He used me. He intended to use God only knows how many others. I killed two people because of him, for him." A low sob emerged from her throat. "I just wanted it all to go away."

"So you set the house on fire."

"Yes." She glanced down at the can in her hand with almost detached amusement. "I didn't have any accelerant back then. I didn't need it. It wasn't like the other night, when I was trying to start the fire from the outside. I just crept into his house while he was sleeping, lit a match and dropped it on the bed. I don't think he ever woke up."

And a town was left to grieve a child molester, while the one woman who might have tried to stop him was left to be forgotten. Maggie nearly shook her head at the awfulness of it.

She stared at the woman before her. "If you felt guilty about what happened to the Rosses, why didn't you confess? If not at the time, then later. You were a child. There were extenuating circumstances. They would have gone easier on you."

"I didn't want anyone to know. I still don't. The idea of having everybody know what I did and why I did it—I couldn't take it. 'Lonely girl gets involved with older man to replace the father figure she doesn't have at home.' The only thing worse than being such a fool is being such a cliché."

Before Maggie could respond, another voice did for her.

"No, being a killer is worse than that. You're not worried about people finding out you're that, I take it?"

He emerged from the shadows like an avenging angel, big, strong and angry. Relief shot through her at the sight of him, the blessed knowledge that he was safe. It was all she could do not to choke out his name.

Sam.

Sam wanted to tell Maggie to run, to get out of this house as fast as she could. He'd already seen on his way through the house from the backyard where Teri had dragged him that the whole lower level was drenched with gasoline. And while the gasoline can was still in her right hand, he could see she had something clutched in her left, something she no doubt intended to use to ignite the gasoline and set the place ablaze.

He didn't bother. As much as he needed her out of here, he didn't believe for a second she would willingly leave the house, especially not if he was in here.

And he wasn't going anywhere.

Not as long as Teri Winslow was here. Not as long as his parents' killer was standing in front of him.

She looked exactly like an older version of the girl he remembered. Tall, skinny, with straight brown hair and glasses. Except this wasn't the same girl who'd laughed and joked and played with him and his brothers, who'd made them snacks while they waited for his parents to come home. No, this woman looked haunted, afraid.

She damn well should be.

"Sam," she said softly, and he realized with a jolt that she knew who he was.

"You know who I am?"

"From the first time I saw you. You look just like your parents."

"My parents who you killed."

"Yes," she said sadly, with a simplicity that only infuriated him further.

"Do you even think about them at all?"

"Every day," she whispered.

"You didn't want people to know why? What about us? Didn't we deserve to know why? Didn't we deserve to understand why our family was destroyed? Didn't we deserve some kind of closure? Didn't you owe us that much after what you did?"

"I couldn't. I wasn't strong enough. I just wanted to forget."

Her words struck an uncomfortable chord. Wasn't that what he'd spent the past thirty years doing? Running? Trying to forget, not strong enough to face what he'd thought he'd done?

Except he hadn't done anything. The knowledge brought no release, only anger that so many years had been wasted, because of his own stupidity and this woman's actions.

He motioned around the room. "Is that what this is about? The gasoline? The fire the other night? The vandalism? The attack on Maggie?"

"Yes," she said. "I just wanted you to stop. I'm still not strong enough. I just want to forget."

She let the can tumble from her fingers to clatter on the floor, the sound from within it indicating there was still some gasoline in it. Some of it began to pour out on the floor, spreading in a pool around her.

She used her newly empty fingers to open the object he could identify in her other hand.

A matchbook.

Before he could react, she'd torn a match from the book and lit it.

"I'm sorry," she whispered.

She dropped the match.

It took less than a heartbeat. The pool of gasoline at her feet burst into flames, the sight so blinding that Sam instinctively raised his arm to block his eyes. When he lowered it, he saw that the fire had already spread all the way around her.

And to her.

Teri was on fire, the flames licking at her pants, soaring up her body, ravenous, unrelenting.

She didn't even scream. That was the most terrifying part. She stood there as the flames engulfed her and didn't even scream. She threw her mouth open and emitted a low, unnerving sound, something that almost sounded like release.

He would have stood there, staring at the horrifying sight, if he hadn't felt Maggie's hand on his arm, yanking on it. "Come on! We have to get out of here!"

She was right, of course. Even as she said it, the fire began to spread with terrifying speed across the floor, following the path of the gasoline.

Without further urging, he finally turned away from Teri and followed Maggie toward the front of the house, racing for the front door and across the lawn until they were a safe distance away.

As soon as they came to a stop, she turned to face him. "Are you all right?"

"I'm fine. You?"

"Okay. When I saw your key on the floor, I thought something must have happened to you."

"She knocked me out, must have dragged me out in the backyard."

"So she didn't want to kill you," Maggie pointed out. "When it came right down to it she couldn't kill again."

"It's a little too late for me to be giving her points for anything, especially when she took the easy way out rather than face the consequences for what she did."

"At least it's over now. We're safe."

They both turned to look at the house, now fully ablaze, a mesmerizing sight against the black night sky. And it *was* over, he realized. His parents' killer had been identified and punished, even if it hadn't been in a method he would have liked. The truth about his own role, or lack of it, in the events of that night had been revealed. And now the house, the source of so many of his nightmares, was vanishing before his eyes.

He suddenly felt lighter than he could ever remember feeling, as though that weight he'd been carrying on his shoulders for so long had finally been removed.

He felt free.

And then it finally hit him. This was Maggie's house, the one she'd fought for with such determination for so long, the one that meant so much to her.

He looked over at her. The eerie glow cast by the

fire illuminated her expression. There was sadness there, although not to the degree he would have expected. It was mostly resignation. "I'm sorry about the house," he said.

She slowly shook her head, never taking her eyes from the inferno. "It was just a house," she said softly. And even though she'd fought to keep it for so long, he felt the truth in her words and knew she meant every one.

Was, she'd said. As though the house were already gone. And it was, he realized, as the last of the shell disintegrated in the flames. The outline of its structure was no longer visible, because it wasn't there. All that remained was the fire.

The house was gone, and with it the past, at long last.

Chapter Eighteen

After the first fire, it had been a relief to see the house in sunlight and discover the damage wasn't as bad as it had seemed it would be in the dark. The light of day was less kind this time, the midday sun shining an unrelenting glow on the charred remains of the structure. There was next to nothing left, the flames having been allowed to consume it all. By the time the volunteer fire department had arrived, the fire having been too severe and gone on too long to be ignored this time, there'd been nothing to do but stomp out the embers.

Strange how quickly something could disappear, Maggie thought. Yesterday, less than twenty-four hours ago, a house had stood here. Now it didn't. Once she'd been married. Then, seemingly in the blink of an eye, she hadn't been. And Sam. It seemed as if just moments ago he'd been standing here in this very spot, by her side.

And now he was gone.

They'd checked back into the motel last night—practically this morning—and collapsed into bed, fully dressed, almost as soon as they stumbled into the room. The last thing she remembered was being curled up beside him, her back to his chest, his arm slung over her. His warmth, his closeness, had blocked out everything else as she finally gave into the exhaustion of everything that had happened yesterday.

He'd been gone when she woke. She would have had to have expected otherwise to be surprised. Instead she'd simply looked at the spot on the mattress where he'd lain, the imprint of his body still on the sheet, then forced herself to get up and start moving, as she'd done before. As she would do again.

His brother's wedding was tomorrow. She knew how badly he wanted to go, and she knew his truck was ready. It made sense that he would want to be on his way. And unlike Kevin, he'd never promised her a thing.

He'd moved on. Now she had to do the same.

If only she had a clue where to go now.

She stared at the remnants of the house, telling herself they were the cause of the heaviness in her chest, nothing else. It would take a great deal of time and effort to rebuild, not to mention far more energy than she had left. Fortunately, it wasn't her problem anymore.

She was so deep in thought that she didn't realize a vehicle had pulled up behind her until she heard a door slam. Startled, she jerked her head toward the noise.

And this time she was surprised. Shocked, really.

Because she hadn't expected it, couldn't quite believe it now that it was happening.

It was Sam.

As she watched, he strode toward her, his eyes steady on her face. He was wearing the same clothes as yesterday, the fabric rumpled, his face unshaven.

No one had ever looked better to her in her entire life.

Her heart thundering in her ears, she gaped at him. When he was a few feet away she blurted out, "What are you doing here?"

"Looking for you, like I've been doing all day. I was even here earlier, but you weren't. For a town this small, I sure seem to have a hard time finding anybody."

"Why?"

He frowned. "Why what?"

"Why were you looking for me?"

"Because I didn't know where you were," he said as though it were the most obvious thing in the world, which it probably was. "You weren't at the motel when I got back."

"Back?" she echoed faintly. "When I woke up, you were gone."

"Nate came by. I didn't think you'd be up for going out, so I went to pick up my truck and get some breakfast. I left you a note on the table."

"I didn't see it." Didn't think to look for one. As soon as she'd seen that he was gone, she'd wanted nothing more than to get out of the motel room and away from all the memories it contained.

"Guess I should have left it on the bed."

Maybe he should have. Or maybe she shouldn't have jumped to conclusions, she thought, heat climbing her cheeks.

When she didn't say anything, he surveyed her through shrewd eyes. "You thought I took off for good."

She shrugged half-heartedly. "Your brother's wedding is tomorrow morning. I figured you needed to get on the road."

"Without saying goodbye?"

"I know how much you've wanted this…"

"Yeah, I do," he admitted. "But I know where he is. I can find him now. But I didn't know where you would go after this. I had a hard enough time finding you in this town. I can only imagine how hard it would be to find you if you left."

"But you don't stick around," she whispered. "You made that clear."

He dipped his head in acknowledgment. "I think I finally found something worth sticking around for. Besides, I'm ready to put the past behind me. It's time."

His face was more relaxed than she'd ever seen it, and she knew he meant every word.

Yes, she agreed silently. Maybe it was time for her, too.

As though reading her thoughts, he glanced toward the nearly empty space where the house once stood.

"What about you? What are you going to do with all of this?"

"I checked with Dalton this morning. He still wants the property. The price he offered still stands, so I took it. I already signed the papers."

"So that's it, then."

"Yeah," she said softly.

"And you're really okay with that?"

"I have to admit, my petty side isn't too happy about letting him get what he wants after all the hassle he gave me, but he didn't seem as if he was gloating when I went to see him. He said he knew how much the house meant to me and he was sorry, and I actually believe he was. I'm sure he'll build a beautiful home on the property, one where people will want to live, and they'll be happy here."

"What about you? Where will you be happy?"

She hesitated, almost afraid to voice the words. Hell, she was terrified. "Wherever you're going."

"I'm going to a wedding. You want to come?"

The breath caught in her throat. A wedding. To see his family for the first time in thirty years. "Are you sure you want me—"

"Yeah," he cut her off. "I'm sure."

She swallowed. "I'd love to."

He gestured with his arm, an "after you" motion that indicated for her to take the first step forward and let him follow. She started to do just that.

Then she paused.

Understanding softened his gaze. "One last look?"

She thought about it, tempted, ready to turn for one last glimpse. Then realization struck. Firm. Undeniable. Freeing.

She shook her head. "I don't need it." And she didn't. It was finally behind her in more ways than one.

With a smile, he offered his hand.

She took it, and together they made their way back to their vehicles, then through town, then beyond, all the way into their future.

She never once looked back.

Epilogue

They were late.

As the clock ticked down to the time the wedding was scheduled to begin Saturday morning and they came closer to their destination in the Adirondacks, Sam almost managed to convince himself they were going to make it. But the mountain chapel where the ceremony was to be held turned out to be a real challenge to find. They had to stop for directions several times, and as they reached the winding road that purportedly led to it, the clock finally hit the designated time.

"Damn," Sam muttered, feeling the air go out of him as he took in the timepiece on the truck's panel.

"It'll be fine," Maggie said with utter calm, as she had numerous times during the drive. Early in their journey, they'd decided to leave her truck in a parking lot and come back for it later. The rightness of having her here had only increased the farther they traveled. It had been nice to just talk in a way they hadn't been able to before now, and even when they'd fallen into silence, it has been an easy, comfortable one. No matter what else happened, staying in Fremont for her hadn't been a mistake.

He could only hope she was right, though. Part of him couldn't ignore the fear that, after so many years of practically ignoring their existence, missing his brother's wedding might be the one final unforgivable sin from which there was no turning back.

That was, if he was even wanted here at all.

The tension was about ready to drive him out of his skin when the road finally plateaued. A small chapel appeared before them, the mountains surrounding it providing a breathtaking backdrop. Several other vehicles were parked in the small lot out front. Sam pulled into a space and quickly climbed out, Maggie doing the same on her side. He didn't have to tell her to hurry or wait for her. She was already matching him step for step as they rushed toward the building.

They came to a stop in front of the double wooden doors. Hoping they could slip in unnoticed, Sam reached for one of the handles, hesitating the slightest moment to suck in a breath, then pulled the door open.

And immediately wished he hadn't. The door opened with a loud squeal of its hinges. He saw instantly that he'd overestimated the size of the chapel. It didn't open onto any kind of lobby, or maybe the tiny space just inside the entryway, barely longer than the length of his arm, was what passed for one.

Instead, the door opened right into the main room

of the chapel. He found himself looking at a wedding, already in progress. A man and a woman standing in front of a minister, facing each other.

The minister stopped in midsentence, the echo of his final words hanging in the air.

Wood groaned as the spectators in the few rows of pews slowly turned to investigate the cause of the interruption. There weren't many of them, he thought, taking them in with a glance, then automatically going back for a second look. Three couples. Three men, three women, one of them with a baby. His brothers. Their…wives? Girlfriends? He didn't know. So much he didn't know…

The couple at the front had both glanced toward the door, as well. Sam didn't even notice the bride, his eyes locked on those of the groom, instantly knowing who he must be.

Gideon.

His face was hard and weathered, lined with age. There was just enough there for Sam to recognize him, but he didn't look like himself, any more than Sam himself must. He looked…old.

He almost laughed at the thought. Sam must look just as old in his eyes, in all of their eyes.

The brief impulse died as he stared at the man's face. He searched it for any indication of what he was thinking. Did he even know who Sam was? After all the years of silence, was Sam even welcome here?

He waited for some sign, some signal, tension knotting in his chest, until he could barely breathe.

Then, though it almost seemed impossible, that

hard face softened slightly. And as his mouth eased in what Sam remembered was his smile, it almost seemed like he was glad to see him. He nodded once. An acknowledgment. A welcome.

Relief and joy burst inside him, nearly buckling his knees. His heart in his throat, Sam couldn't move. Needing a lifeline, he did the only thing he could.

He reached for her hand.

He didn't have to reach far. It was already there, open and waiting for his.

Maggie gave his fingers a reassuring squeeze, and he felt the tightness in his chest ease the slightest bit. Just enough that he could breathe and do what he needed to do.

He took a step forward.

Beside him, Maggie did just as he did, so they were moving as one.

And together they walked inside to finally join the others.

* * * * *

Harlequin offers a romance for every mood!
See below for a sneak peek from our
suspense romance line
Silhouette® Romantic Suspense.
Introducing HER HERO IN HIDING by
New York Times *bestselling author Rachel Lee.*

Kay Young returned to woozy consciousness to find that she was lying on a soft sofa beneath a heap of quilts near a cheerfully burning fire. When she tried to move, however, everything hurt, and she groaned.

At once she heard a sound, then a stranger with a hard, harsh face was squatting beside her. "Shh," he said softly. "You're safe here. I promise."

"I have to go," she said weakly, struggling against pain. "He'll find me. He can't find me."

"Easy, lady," he said quietly. "You're hurt. No one's going to find you here."

"He will," she said desperately, terror clutching at her insides. "He always finds me!"

"Easy," he said again. "There's a blizzard outside. No one's getting here tonight, not even the doctor. I know, because I tried."

"Doctor? I don't need a doctor! I've got to get away."

"There's nowhere to go tonight," he said levelly. "And if I thought you could stand, I'd take you to a window and show you."

But even as she tried once more to pull away the quilts, she remembered something else: this man had been gentle when he'd found her beside the road, even when she had kicked and clawed. He hadn't hurt her.

Terror receded just a bit. She looked at him and detected signs of true concern there.

The terror eased another notch and she let her head sag on the pillow. "He always finds me," she whispered.

"Not here. Not tonight. That much I can guarantee."

Will Kay's mysterious rescuer protect her
from her worst fears?
Find out in HER HERO IN HIDING *by* New York Times *bestselling author Rachel Lee.*
Available June 2010,
only from Silhouette® Romantic Suspense.

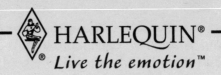

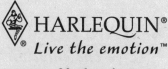

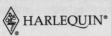

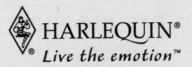

Love Inspired SUSPENSE
RIVETING INSPIRATIONAL ROMANCE

Watch for our new series of
edge-of-your-seat suspense novels.
These contemporary tales
of intrigue and romance
feature Christian characters
facing challenges to their faith...
and their lives!

NOW AVAILABLE IN REGULAR & LARGER-PRINT FORMATS

Steeple
Hill®

Visit:
www.SteepleHill.com

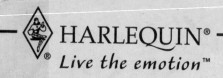

Harlequin® Historical
Historical Romantic Adventure!

*Imagine a time of chivalrous
knights and unconventional ladies,
roguish rakes and impetuous
heiresses, rugged cowboys
and spirited frontierswomen—
these rich and vivid tales will
capture your imagination!*

*Harlequin Historical . . .
they're too good to miss!*

HARLEQUIN®

Super Romance®

...there's more to the story!

Superromance.
A *big* satisfying read about unforgettable
characters. Each month we offer *six* very different
stories that range from family drama to adventure
and mystery, from highly emotional stories to
romantic comedies—and much more! Stories
about people you'll believe in and care about.
Stories too compelling to put down....

Our authors are among today's *best* romance
writers. You'll find familiar names and talented
newcomers. Many of them are award winners—
and you'll see why!

If you want the biggest and best
in romance fiction, you'll get it
from Superromance!

Exciting, Emotional, Unexpected...

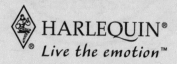

HARLEQUIN®
Live the emotion™